Chap

Emily Paige may have defied the status quo by becoming a woman carpenter, but she couldn't defy the law of gravity. The warning creak came too late, the floorboards collapsed…then Emily whooshed through the jagged hole.

Ouch! That hurt.

Her head and the wood splinters above it swirled in a stream of morning light. God almighty! How does a floor cave in? Thankfully the tub held on. To what? That beautiful antiquated, lion-clawed – weighs more than a Hummer – tub!

She could have been crushed! Well, the thought hurt worse than the fall. A sideways motion, to spill out of the way, left her woozy. Lying back down, five feet off the ground, gratitude sunk in. She fingered the cool, grey stack of gyprock beneath her. Wiggling extremities, with no ill effects, an audible sigh pursed the dust laden air.

No broken bones.

Yup…should have listened to Joe. This wasn't a fixer-upper. It was a vampire.

Just waiting to suck you dry. I can see all sorts of unexpected pitfalls and ghastly expenses coming your way.

Well, he was the expert. He'd be insulted if she didn't ask his opinion. Joe was her brother-in-law in Maine's thriving city of Portland. Not that she took his advice. Emily raced to buy the wreck of a home on the most beautiful property on Oak Boulevard. No time to think it through.

"If only he could see me now," she muttered. "Pitfalls certainly are a pain in the ass." Sliding down the pile of construction material she was relieved to see that only the top few boards sustained damage; other than a spot on her tail bone that throbbed, eliciting a rub.

"Going to the movies? Caught you picking your seat!" Caitlyn Tosh's cherry voice jarred her around like a spin top. And, as always, her infectious smile managed to riddle Emily's caustic mood with holes.

"Hey Cait'. What are you doing here?" She grinned, flicking at an array of splinters that clung to her auburn bangs.

"Jenny is opening for me this morning. Made enough ca-ching! over the summer to hire her full-time, remember?"

"Right. Business is booming. So, what's up?"

"Just running a few errands. You forgot your coffee. And, since you bought a nuker for the kitchen here, I figured you could warm it up. Save you a trip away from all…this." Caitlyn swept an arm through the dust laden air, her appraising glances settling on the hole overhead. "That doesn't look good."

Emily stretched up on her leather clad toes then let her body go limp. She linked her fingers and leaned back, effectively dissolving the last few kinks in her neck and shoulders.

"I just found out the bathroom floor needs to be replaced. Luckily, I had gyprock for the kitchen delivered yesterday, and this is where they piled it. Broke my fall."

"Holy Shit! You could have been seriously hurt. You *sure* you still want to take this on?" Caitlyn reached for her arm. "It could end up costing a lot more than just money you know."

Emily appreciated her friend's concern but backing out now was not an option. She'd settled the financing and paperwork a week ago. How had she missed that floor damage?

Thinking back there had been a broadloom rug on the wooden floor the day she viewed the dwelling for the first time. She had to admit it was a renovator's nightmare, increasingly so. But the house had beautiful bones. The kind Emily couldn't ignore once the century old brownstone appeared in the Bangor realty listings.

Besides, living in Bangor meant only a two hour drive to Joe and her sister Hillary's home in Portland. It was important to stay close to family, with enough distance to assert her independence. She vowed to make it on her own.

Or die trying.

"Okay, you're right. I do need some help. I'll look in the yellow pages...today," she added, catching a heard-that-one-before look.

"Great! I have to say, I envy the tan you're getting with all the outside work you've managed to do." Caitlyn let go of her arm and reached for a hug. "Gotta run. Your coffee is in the kitchen. I came in through the back. Have fun!"

"Thanks, Cait'. See you tonight." Emily gave an extra squeeze then followed her best friend's lanky frame to the battered front door.

"Just do it!" Caitlyn's final salute flew over a lily white shoulder. She bounced gingerly down the makeshift ramp – a temporary fix for a disintegrating wooden staircase – and slid into a vintage 1970's Dodge Charger. Its new purple paint job matched the spikey tips of her short blond hair. Emily had to grin. At least they both appreciated antiquity.

Her blue smile flipped over as a poppy red Jeep pulled up to the curb on the opposite side of Oak Boulevard.

Now what?

The man sitting inside caught her gaze. Aviator sunglasses, salt-and-pepper hair, face – indistinguishable. She could roughly discern his mouth. Jaw set tight. Rigid, really. Was he glaring? At the sold sticker plastered across Empire Realty's requisite marketing board, she assumed. Relenting to Sid Sousa, her realtor, the sign would remain until the end of the month.

Fine! But she couldn't wait to yank it out. One more thing that didn't require a man. One more thing she wouldn't have to pay someone to do.

Emily closed the front door, then ducked into the living room. A large wooden window provided the perfect vantage point from which to study the man who was studying her property sign. A moment later he stepped onto the road. An easy gait and long, muscular legs ate up the distance to Empire's signpost in the time it took Emily to fully inhale.

What was this hunk of testosterone doing on her property? Her pupils grew larger when the tall stranger stuck a scrap of paper to the realty sign and quickly retreated. Taking command of the Jeep, he steered away, in the opposite direction of the Charger, away from the city.

She turned to glare at the hole in her ceiling and the stack of gyprock below. A mountain of work confronted her. "Ka-ching!" Emily snapped at the crushed board.

She read the wording twice before crumpling the page and tossing it into the fireplace. Not that it worked. To bring it up to code, a new steel liner needed to be installed. Thankfully, the previous owners fixed the chimney's brickwork. Of course they had used wood for heat – the oil tank outside resembled an oversized bucket of rust. She would have to replace it before winter arrived. The stranger's note lingered in her mind.

If you decide to sell, please let me know ASAP. I can't believe I missed this opportunity and I'm willing to pay over market price.

Best regards, Ben.

There was a phone number, no last name, no address. Not what she expected. Although it didn't surprised her. Emily hadn't dickered on the price of her diamond in the rough.

Okay, perhaps an unpolished beach stone more aptly described her current investment, but she couldn't overlook the potential! Besides, if funds ran out before completing the renovation, an interested party wanted the property. That in itself offered some relief to the tide of misfortunes that threatened to drown her resolve.

Just do it!

Her new mantra. She strut off to the kitchen with purpose in search of a phonebook and to retrieve the coffee Caitlyn had thoughtfully brought over. Meaning to zap some heat into the now tepid beverage, she picked up the cord of a small, white microwave oven and plugged it in. Sparks hissed and spewed like a birthday cake sparkler.

Damn it! She yanked out the plug and felt a wave of despair slosh over her. Tradesmen, including electricians, didn't come cheap. Perhaps she should keep the mystery man's phone number.

You know, just in case.

Ben swept his steely blue eyes over the downtrodden brownstone and settled on a curvy figure in the open doorway. So that's who snapped up the property on his most wanted list. Boy, she looked mean in a black tank top, thread-bare cutoffs and work boots. A mustard colored work belt hugged her hips. With auburn brown curls escaping a high ponytail and teasing an oval shaped face, he had to admit, she looked smoking hot as well.

If only he could get a closer look. He'd driven by Wednesday morning. Just to check on her progress. Perhaps she would find the restoration too arduous and decide to dump the property right away. But she hadn't. A week later and she was still there slugging it out – alone. He'd not seen a man on the property, not that it mattered. He had only driven by three times himself so there had been plenty of opportunity for other men to be helping out. Maybe she was a tradesperson herself and didn't need a man. Ben let out an involuntary chuckle. "Yeah, right," he muttered with a shake of his head and a straight-lipped grin.

As much as he admitted defeat in losing out on an incredible opportunity, he just couldn't let it go. If she did decide to pack it in, and she could, it was still early in the game. He needed her to know he would relieve her the burden of that brownstone deed in a heartbeat.

It took a scant moment to scribble a message in the notebook by his side and tear out the page. After tacking it to a realtor's sign on the edge of a lawn-under-repair, he sped away. No other unfinished business in Bangor. Nothing to hang around for.

Ben pulled a U-turn and head back to Oak Boulevard exactly three minutes later. Living by the old wait-and-see rule was not working for him. He'd had enough disappointments with that precept. High time he took charge and made something happen – like getting that little hottie to accept his offer.

He careened up to the curb. Time to dust off the old Blackheart charisma. In the past, women he chose to flatter fell for him like autumn leaves in a wind storm. Too easy.

With determined strides he ignored the flimsy front ramp and circled to the backyard. The view when he round the corner stopped him cold.

Ass crack – he didn't expect that, or the dainty, pink thong peeking out from the back of her jean shorts. Then he noticed the lawnmower. The woman crouching beside it jabbed at a small black, rubber bubble.

"Easy ma'am, you're going to flood that thing all to hell." Ben turned away from the heated glare that whipped around to face him. "Bad choice of words. Sorry about that."

She stood and turned on him, meaner than a tank engine, with steam blowing out of her cute little ears. "Ma'am? Do I look like a ma'am to you?" she spat.

So much for the old Blackheart charm. "No ma'am…" Ben flailed to correct his terminology. "I mean miss! Actually, you look pretty hot, work boots and all." The hint of a smile from the distraught woman ground him with hope. Hope that was doomed the minute she spoke.

"I have a lot of work to do as you can see and the day is getting hotter by the minute. I'd like to get the lawns mowed and watered before they turn to dust, so if there's something you want, spit it out. I'm busy."

You! The thought shot through his brain like a bullet. Not that he would tell *her* that. But if he didn't do, or say, something soon, his feelings would become all too apparent. Ben crossed his hands in front of himself and nodded towards the stone-clad dwelling.

"I want this house," he said dryly. "Had my eye on it for a while now. I had a feeling it would come to market soon. Of course, with the amount of work it needs, I didn't think there would be any serious competition. But, here you've gone and bought it out from underneath me." He dared a glance in her direction.

Taut lips curled into a wistful pout. "Do you always get what you want?"

He grit his teeth. "Not always. But, I get what I need."

Emily cocked her head and raised her brow, a plea for elucidation, so he continued. "I didn't get to put an offer in on this beauty, so I didn't get what I want. But I don't need it either. I'm up to my ears in work now. It's just that. Well, I always keep an eye out for a...for projects."

Ben valued his privacy. Wary of Miss Spitfire's mental acuity, he didn't want to say too much. Perhaps there was a good explanation for her mean streak. Could be having a bad day. Once the fire left those dark brown eyes, her childlike aura enchanted him. He could get used to that. "I didn't get your name."

"You didn't ask."

"I'd like to know more about you."

Her voice softened a notch. "Emily Paige. And you are?"

He stepped forward and extended his right hand. "Benjamin Blackheart. I go by Ben. Nice to meet you, Emily." He liked the way her name rolled off his tongue. She ignored his hand, but held his gaze. "Well, I guess I should make good on my offer to buy this old derelict from you."

"Don't waste your breath. The answer is no." Emily crossed arms under a damp bosom.

To his chagrin, the gesture reignited his desire. The V-shape rising from the scooped neck of her tank top beaded with perspiration. Ben lowered his gaze to her grass stained knees. Better. "Well, if you change your mind, you have my number."

"I do. Thanks." She turned back to the lawnmower.

Ben frowned, still wanting to see inside the brownstone. In the moment he lingered on that thought, Emily yanked on a frayed starter cord. The cord whipped out of the machine when it snapped. She screamed. Ben dove to prevent her fall, catching the full brunt of her elbow…in his face.

Chapter Two

Ouch! That hurt.

Ben would have laughed if his cheek didn't ache so much. Not what he expected, or hoped for, but she did fall for him. Right into his arms no less. Not that it would ever happen again. The woman didn't so much as offer him an icepack after bashing him in the face with her elbow. He would have been happy with a bag of frozen peas. Though she did apologize profusely when his cheek bone swelled and turned an angry red color.

Her doing.

Well, he'd had enough abuse for one day, and having made sure *she* was okay, he left. Tires screeching down the street, he couldn't wait to get away. Forget about Emily – forget the brownstone too. Wait and see. With any luck, another restoration project would turn up, nowhere near Oak Boulevard.

He still needed an older, energy sucking house to renovate. It would showcase his work eventually and help attract the local population. Not that he disliked designing unique, eco-friendly estates for the rich and famous. But, that caliber of clientele was nonexistent near his home in rural Wesley. Work inevitably required travel, at times taking him abroad – the European market proved to be especially lucrative.

However, his long-term plan for Blackheart Designs included energy saving and eco-friendly solutions for the renovation market. And the urgency to find clientele closer to home grew in spades since his father's death. With no siblings around to pitch in, Ava, his mother, needed him more than ever. Thankfully, their homes shared a property line and the same private road, so he could keep a close eye on her.

Initially, Ben chose Bangor to showcase his talent. The city's sprawling urban population and proximity to home made it the ideal location. Come the weekend, he'd be driving to Portland for a final meeting with clients. Bangor stood closer to home, but he was beginning to think the longer drive would be worth it. Especially if it meant not having to worry about coming face to face with Emily Paige one more time.

After the coming weekend, after the nice couple in Portland signed off on the design for their new estate, his slate would be clear to pursue the masses. He made a mental note to check the Portland realty listings when he arrived home. He'd take another look at Bangor too.

You know, just in case.

Chapter Three

Emily hopped into her little blue Colt, tapped the dash and cranked the engine. After four years on the road, it still ran pretty darn good. She drove out of her designated parking space and turned the car towards Portland. This evening's celebration dinner with Hillary and Joe would be a welcome end to a grueling week. They invited Caitlyn as well, but she'd given Jenny Sunday off to attend a friend's wedding.

That's the problem with running a business, thought Emily – no *real* downtime. Caitlyn owned The Hungry Owl, a café, slash, new and used book store. The regulars alone allowed her to maintain a thriving business. The one annoyance – having a social life buttonholed by work obligations.

The situation reaffirmed Emily's decision to keep her job as a contributing writer for Outdoor American. She valued her free time. Once the magazine's senior editor approved the final copy of a story assignment, Emily could go back to working on a house flip. She had the best of both worlds.

Hillary, her only sister, had the *best* of one world, one she thrived in – domesticity. While she baked cookies with mother and played house with dolls, Emily had been daddy's girl. To her, the woodsy aroma coaxed from a planer or saw was nirvana.

It wasn't long before she had free reign with her father's arsenal of woodworking tools. Under close supervision at first. Emily's mother received countless handmade birdhouses as gifts over the years. After the first few, they didn't suck anymore. At seventeen Emily could nail down hardwood floors and trim out a small bungalow without assistance. Samuel Paige had been proud of his daughter's carpentry skills, but urged her to pursue less strenuous work. In fact, one of their last conversations centered on future career goals.

You're a good writer. Straight A's in English from the time you started school. Have you ever stopped to consider writing for a living?

No, not ever. But she did promise to think about it.

Things changed after the accident. Lots of things. Like suddenly, the Paige girls were on their own. Only Hillary had a wide circle of girlfriends and a devoted boyfriend, Joe, to help ease the loss. Maternal instincts developed overnight. Emily found herself living with a fiercely protective older sister, and Joe.

What might he say after hearing the latest renovation report? *I told you so,* topped the list. She anticipated Hillary's reaction as well. *You should come home. It's too much for you by yourself.*

Emily shuddered. The thought of moving back to Portland gave her chills. Especially when driving past the stretch of highway that her parents died on. Too many painful memories. She could never be happy living in Portland.

Thankfully, tonight was not a catch-up dinner to find out how little sister was doing. This evening would be all about Hillary, Joe and their new estate plans. If she remembered correctly, they had invited a guest to dinner as well. She had a good chance of staying out of the limelight. Perhaps no one would ask how the renovation was going.

"The renovations are going beautifully," said Emily. Both women knew it was a lie. Hillary could read her little sister like a book. She looked away and made a lame comment about the weather. It was enough to tamp down the emotional dread that ebbed beneath her skin. She forced a smile and turned back to her older sister. "I

"Call me tonight after you get home okay. I know you don't want to air your troubles in front of company. We'll talk about it later. And if there's anything we can do to help, I want you to let me know."

Emily promised to call. No big deal. She called her sister after every visit to let them know she made it home, all in one piece.

"Very well. Come help me with dinner. I think it's time to test the wine."

Emily took her wink to mean the wine didn't really need testing. "Good idea," she said, playing along. "You never know. We may have to adjust the temperature. Is it red or white?"

"We have both. Joe picked up a bunch of fresh seafood on his way home. It's not considered gauche to drink red wine with fish anymore you know."

"Great, I could really use a drink of something stronger than spring water right now. It's been one hell of a week." Emily followed Hillary into the kitchen where a selection of wine glasses stood sparkling clean on the counter.

A thump on the cool ceramic floor tiles caught her attention. She veered over to a doggie bed in the corner and bent to pat a rather large Irish setter. Sinking her fingers into his silky red fur, she cooed. "Hey, Finnegan. Where's your daddy?" The thumping tail went into overdrive and Finnegan nuzzled his chin against her bare knees. As a rule, Emily didn't wear dresses. She chose one today for Hillary's sake, or that of her company. An approving smile from her sister confirmed she'd made the right choice in wearing her light yellow frock.

"Joe's up showering. He'll be down in a minute. I have to change before Benny arrives, but other than that I'm ready to celebrate." Happiness resonated in Hillary's voice.

"Who did you say was coming? I don't think I caught the name."

The doorbell chimed.

"Shoot! He's early." Hillary abandoned the bottle of wine she'd been uncorking and dashed out of the kitchen.

"I got it!" Joe yelled.

Bare feet thumped down the hardwood stairs while Hillary disappeared. Then the front door opened and Joe's baritone voice carried through to the kitchen with the weight of steamroller. "Hey, Ben! Good grief, man. What happened to you?"

She didn't hear his response. The box of sea salt in her hand suddenly dropped, hit a stainless-steel pot lid on the counter and produced an earsplitting clang. She swallowed hard.

It couldn't be.

Emily had never been a math whiz, but she could put two and two together. Hillary and Joe's architect was some hot-shot who designed one-of-a-kind green living solutions. She'd been to visit the new lakefront property on four occasions over the summer. Apparently, she missed running into him each time and big sister kept saying what a shame it was. How, Emily couldn't fathom.

Hillary said that Ben's work seduced environmentalists around the globe. The Graftons considered themselves lucky to have secured his services. There was a catch. Ben was prematurely gray and wore his hair long. Emily couldn't imagine wanting anything to do with him. Not that a little grey hair meant much, but in her head she pictured a man too mature for her liking.

"You're not getting any younger, sis," Hillary chimed in exasperation when she'd voiced her objections. "You don't go to church and you abhor the bar scene. I don't blame you. But instead of the gym, you do yoga in your living room and go for long runs by yourself. You'll never meet a man to your liking if all you do is work."

Emily had winced at that comment. Hillary was right. Fierce independence and limited social interactions did restrict meeting eligible members of the opposite sex.

Her pulse quickened as Joe led their guest to the dining area off the kitchen. "Emily Paige, this is Benjamin Blackheart, our designer and…ah Ben, this is Emily, Hillary's sister."

The look of shock in his steely blue eyes sent shivers down her spine despite the heat. She remembered the screech of his tires as he tore away from her house on Oak Boulevard. How embarrassed and sorry she had felt after he left. Especially since the ice compartment of her refrigerator couldn't make slush, let alone produce a tray of ice cubes. She'd nothing to offer but apologies after nearly knocking him out with her elbow.

His eye color had been a mystery. They'd been covered by those large, reflective sunglasses the whole time. What was it – five minutes? Enough time for her to make a complete ass of herself.

"Hello." It was Joe. His voice cut the awkward silence as effectively as a director who had just yelled, 'Action!'

Everyone moved at once. Emily took a tentative step forward and this time she took Ben's hand when he extended it. When she pulled away, he tightened his grip on her hand. Joe had taken over the job of uncorking wine. If her brother-in-law detected anything amiss in the scene, it didn't show.

"Nice to meet you, Emily." He relaxed his hold, just a little. "So, you're Hillary's little sister. She told me about you."

He didn't give her away. She would have to thank him later, if they managed to catch a moment alone. Looking at him now, Emily wished she could do a whole lot more with Ben than a moment alone would allow. "My pleasure. Please, have a seat."

Ben saw a whole new woman in Emily now as she lowered her gaze and nodded towards a chair at the dining room table. Miss Spitfire had a tame side after all. He loosened his grip on her hand. It felt small and soft in his own.

They were just sitting down when Hillary breezed into the room wearing heels and a red silk dress. Knowing she would be curious, he quickly offered an excuse for the greenish-blue stain on the left side of his face "I walked into a cupboard door that I foolishly left open in my kitchen." He hated to lie, but he could tell Emily was uncomfortable and probably embarrassed considering her behavior when they first met.

He felt a measure of relief when Hillary bent to give him a hug and planted quick gentle kisses on both of his cheeks. For the rest of the evening, however, he was covertly aware of Emily – every movement, every word that came from her shapely, full lips.

The conversation remained light, Joe talking about his day, running the Portland-based construction company that too bore his name. All his summer hiccups were cured. Settling on a location for its next subdivision seemed to be the biggest problem facing Grafton Construction.

Ben stole another glance at Emily while Hillary took a loaf of French bread from the oven. She toyed with the rim of her stemmed glass, going round and round the edge with her index finger. He took note of her jewelry. It was casual – a simple embossed silver band on the ring finger of each hand, the left one bearing a small turquoise stone. No diamonds, no gold band.

The conversation segued to the lakeside property Joe and Hillary bought to build their dream home on. Ben did what he could to pay attention to the banter.

"Hillary wants to add a butterfly garden already and we haven't even broken ground for the house yet. She's always miles ahead of me," said Joe, giving his wife a smile and a wink.

She tugged on his ear and kissed him. "Oh, who cares? At least we're always on the same path." Hillary passed her husband a basket of fragrant, warm bread, then instructed Ben to pour the wine.

"You're like family now, Benny. So, don't expect to be catered to any longer." Everyone could see she was teasing. "We got to know you over the summer planning our dream home. We don't want you to think the kinship we feel toward you is over when we sign off on the plans. You know you're always welcome."

Such a nice family, thought Ben. He picked up the Merlot and turned to Emily. She nodded toward her glass. "Yes, please."

Was that a blush? Ben quickly filled the rest of the stemware.

"Emily brought dessert," announced Hillary when they'd finished the main course. She had just poured everyone a round of freshly brewed coffee.

"It's a Caitlyn creation," admitted Emily.

"You'll have to thank her for us. It looks incredible," said Hillary as she brought a glazed peach pie to the table. "Oh, and

Benny, thank you for the deer steaks you brought us on your last visit. They were delicious."

Joe nodded in agreement. "I was surprised at how tender they were. Best I've eaten."

"You're quite welcome. With hunting season coming up, I needed to make room in the freezer. I'll bring you some fresh steaks next time."

Emily wanted to know where the deer came from. Her curiosity surprised Ben and everyone seemed eager to hear his story, so he obliged sparing few details. He told them about his trek through the forest, the battle of wits as the sturdy buck backtracked and crossed paths in an effort to throw the hunter off his trail.

"But you did find him, didn't you?" Emily interjected.

It wasn't the most riveting story he could have told, but he did appreciate this woman's interest. And other things about her. He turned to face Emily and grinned.

"I tired him, more aptly," said Ben. "When he was worn out, and unable to run anymore, I was able to get close enough for a kill shot. I would hate to wound an animal and have it suffer…even for a minute."

Having come to the end of his story, Ben popped a last piece of pie crust into his mouth and washed it down with the rest of his coffee. After the meal, he rose, intent on helping with the cleanup, but Emily pushed him down in his chair. She cleared the dishes then proceeded to whisk crumbs off the blue damask tablecloth. When she reached across him with a miniature hand broom he almost came undone. Just the scent of her kicked his libido into gear. Keeping it in neutral was becoming next to impossible.

Joe filled the dishwasher while Hillary sat and engaged him in further conversation. He welcomed the distraction. She wanted to talk about solar energy, the main source they would employ in their new home. She wanted to know the timeframe for building, what time of year the trees for a natural windbreak should be planted, which energy efficient appliances to buy. By the time he'd answered her questions the kitchen was clean.

Emily said she hated to leave, but she had a story to finish for some magazine she wrote for. Something about Maine's famous – or was it infamous – hiking trails. Apparently, he'd begun to pay more attention to her lips than the words coming out of them.

In present company, she was sheer delight. Relaxed, domestic and sexier than any woman had a right to be. Unless, perhaps, she was a stripper. He wondered if she had any other side jobs. Not that he cared. Why should he? He would probably never see her again. The Graftons had only to sign the paperwork and hand him a cheque. His work there was done.

On his return trip Ben focused on the road, on the strum of the eighties' tune wafting from the car stereo, on the client list he needed to run through. He wondered how Ava, his mother was fairing at home. What would the proud matriarch think of Emily?

Ben shook his head and blew out a deep breath. He didn't need a woman. He had gotten along fine without one since Doris left. For good this time. Doris King been his girlfriend for nearly a decade.

Great!

Now he had two women on his mind. The latter he found easier to forget.

Emily's look of mortification when he walked into the Grafton's home was etched in his brain. He'd actually felt sorry for her. Over the summer, he had gotten to know her sister and brother-in-law. He counted almost a dozen consultations and several site visits. Joe hadn't been able to make it to them all, but Hillary was fully immersed in the project. Indeed, she could parlay on any topic concerning it with ease. The Graftons were nice people – a nice family, thought Ben.

Darkness prevailed when he reached the outskirts of Bangor. Rolling down the window allowed the cool night air to rush over him. Ben's thoughts still raced in several directions, each one leading back to Emily. From a rise on the highway, he scanned the canopy of city lights and wondered which district housed her apartment building.

One more hour and home would beckon near the quaint little hamlet of Wesley. He played out his nightly routine to keep his mind from wandering again. He pictured his mother's house at the end of the lane. Checking in on her at night became habit. If she was still up they could enjoy a nightcap. A shot of Dalwhinnie or Glenmorangie to warm the blood. He'd check on his laying hens roosting in their coop. Then Jack, his Bluetick hound, would follow him home and they'd settle in for the night. Jack was a Christmas present five years prior, from his father.

"What do you give a guy who has everything?" Donald Blackheart had asked. "You always wanted a dog growing up, but we moved around so much it didn't seem fair to keep an animal. You're thirty-five now, and apparently you're not going anywhere, so here...take good care of him. Name's Jack."

A picture of Emily patting Finnegan came to mind. Their adoration was clearly mutual. The dog whined when she picked up her purse to leave. She would get along just fine with Jack. They were both so...so loveable. Ben shook his head – quick and hard, as if by doing so memories of Emily would dislodge and escape through the open window.

Forget Emily, he told himself for the hundredth time that night. Forget her shy smiles and her easy blush. Forget her long flowing mane of auburn hair, her bright eyes the color of rich, dark chocolate. Forget her luscious lips, her breath as sweet as honey when she bent to whisper in his ear.

What did she say?

"Don't say no to seconds...Hillary will be insulted." Then she piled another heaping scoop of steamed mussels into his bowl and placed another piece of garlic bread on his plate. He remembered the warm smile, the brush of her leg as she settled in the seat beside him.

Outdoor American – he suddenly recalled the name of the magazine Emily wrote for. It had been on the shelves of the drugstore where he picked up Ava's prescriptions. He may have glanced through the publication once while browsing for an almanac. Envisioning the sorry looking patch of corn in his field, he wondered if it would be wise to plow it under and plant pole beans there instead next year. He wondered if Emily knew anything about gardening.

Emily! Why couldn't he just forget about Emily? He reached the service road leading into his property. A thick blanket of cloud held the moon and the stars at bay. Ben rolled his window all the way down and slowed his Jeep to a crawl. Near midnight, in almost complete darkness, there was still the risk of hitting deer should one bolt across his path.

Had it been closer to dusk he would have encountered at least a dozen white tails grazing near roadside pastures. The locals gave deer a wide berth when travelling. Even so, many of Wesley's citizens drove cars marred by dented fenders and cracked windshields, evidence of the creatures' skittish and unpredictable nature.

A single light shone in the window of Ava's house when he pulled into her driveway. Ben turned off his motor and went inside. He needed a scotch. He didn't need a woman, he told himself again.

Chapter Four

Friday, the fourth day of October, was a telling day for Emily. The wind, howling outside, told her to wear a jacket. A desktop calendar indicated she was running out of time. Then a call to Gloria Steinburg confirmed a forthcoming deadline for *Hallowed Hikers*.

Great! Today also happened to be the last day of employment for Tyrone Biggs' geriatric secretary. The astute owner of Outdoor American expected everyone to be in-house at lunch for a farewell party. Handsome beyond words, Tyrone had been the object of many nighttime fantasies during her first year of employment.

She decided to wait out the morning rush hour and arrived at the downtown office building by a quarter to ten. Tyrone noted her impending deadline and took the opportunity to furnish her with another story assignment. "Hunting season is upon us. Come up with something that will appeal to the outdoorsman in everyone! Due in three weeks." He turned on his heel, then pivoted back towards her with the grace of dancer. An erotic dancer, thought Emily.

"By the way…."

"Yes?" Her heart leapt. Was he finally going to ask her out? She held her breath. Cocktails after work would be lovely.

"Good job on that last assignment. It was…impressive." Emily gazed up at him and stuck an appreciative smile on her face. The sheen melted from her eyes as he turned to leave.

Crap! What would it take to get him to *really* notice her? Not that she didn't appreciate his pat on the back, but after a year, she had been hoping for a little more personal attention.

Tyrone strolled away from the cubicles smiling and nodding at colleagues. Emily torpedoed a broken pencil into a nearby trash bin and pushed her glossy lips into a childish pout. Hunting? I don't know anything about hunting, she thought with dismay.

Of course, she didn't know much about magazine writing either, until Tyrone *discovered* her. The decline in newspaper advertising, and hence content, created fierce competition for writing assignments. Hundreds of applicants vied for a handful of jobs when they did pop up.

But then Tyrone read her feature story in the Portland Daily News. After the holiday weekend in July, he called her personally to offer an assignment. She literally jumped at the opportunity, managing to spill a full glass of ice water in her lap when she heard his silky smooth voice on her phone line. The cooling effect was temporary. Women on staff openly drooled over him. However, in the course of her employment, he'd been nothing but a perfect gentleman. It maddened her.

Research through the office grapevine provided his age and status. Tyrone was single and thirty-six, only four years older than Emily. After seeing family photos in his office, she decided that he was the product of a handsomely infused gene pool. And further, by the way his muscles rippled under exquisite raw, silk shirts, a lifetime devotion to gym memberships.

The first opportunity to step outside the confines of business decorum came at lunch, during the retirement party. Carla Stewart had done her time in Maine and was moving back to Florida, her home state. Close to twenty people jammed the staff lounge to congratulate her and extend best wishes.

Allowing time to gauge opportunities before approaching Tyrone, Emily hung back. He'd been talking non-stop with adoring staff members. That made it more difficult to simply walk up and ask him out. *Perhaps we could go for a drink after work, or maybe unwind by taking in a movie or dinner or...*

An unexpected tap on the shoulder squashed her next fantasy.

"Pardon me," crooned Andy Wong, a clerk from the fact checking department. "But did you know he's gay?" He laid his head on Emily's shoulder and batted long black lashes in Tyrone's direction. "You haven't taken your eyes off him since you entered the room."

Andy, as everyone knew, *was out*, always had been and proud of it. He was the life of every social event and everyone's friend. Emily adored him.

She learned that Tyrone kept his sexual preference private, so as not to risk sales of the magazine. Sure it was aimed at active outdoor-loving Americans. But he knew there was still a lot of prejudice in the typical outdoor macho realm. His affairs were few. Fewer still were the people who knew about them.

"And you know because?" Emily blushed at her next thought.

"Oh my, you poor thing. Watch closely princess." Wong winked mischievously at her and carried on.

As he sidled up beside the magazine mogul on the outside of the circle of well-wishers, he reached across and patted his shoulder to garner attention. Then he let his hand travel down Tyrone's back stopping to give his exquisitely chiseled ass a quick squeeze.

"Unbelievable," Emily muttered, heading for the doorway. She would have to reenter the party and appear to have just arrived to protect Andy from his blatant indiscretion.

By the time she reappeared, Carla was crying, having read the group card scrawled with her comrades' parting words. Some lovely farewell gifts, a diamond studded watch and a small Maud Lewis print in a hardwood frame, would accompany her to Florida.

Emily caught Tyrone's welcoming smile as she joined the fray. So, she impressed the boss man. Big deal! She made a mental note then and there to start dating again. At least treat herself to a movie now and then. Maybe try that dating website Caitlyn was so crazy about. Eeew! She cringed at that thought.

After working on renovations for most of the day, Emily spent Saturday evening toying with an outline for the hunting issue. She didn't know any hunters. Well, maybe one, but she'd be damned if she would ask him for any help. For a moment she wondered why the assignment didn't go to one of the male interns. Right. The lot of them, not that there were many, were metro-men. Suits with buffed finger nails.

Perhaps, she mused, this was a test of her versatility. Well, she'd show them. Joe and Hillary were coming in the morning to see if they could do anything to help with her renovation project. Her brother-in-law must have friends who hunted that she could interview. The least she could do was ask. In any event, she was pretty sure there must be some alternative to Ben, whom she'd treated so rudely. She was sure he wouldn't give her the time of day, let alone an interview for a full feature story.

Chapter Five

"There isn't anyone else. I'm quite positive," said Joe, slicking a hand through his mop of dirty blond hair. "Have you tried the gun shops?"

"I called in on a few, but no one would commit to doing an interview with me right away. They're all too busy with hunting season coming up." Emily was at her wits end and she could tell Joe and Hillary were running low on patience with her as well. After giving up their Sunday to help with re-boarding the kitchen walls, they were tired and wanting to get back to Portland.

"I still don't see why you can't just call Benny," Hillary said plaintively. "He said he was taking a break from work after finishing our estate plans. He could probably spare you the time."

He'd probably rather shoot me. The thought made Emily wince and she truly believed it. "I don't know. I'm sure he must have plans for his time off. I'd hate to intrude on him."

"Call him!" the Grafton's shouted in unison.

"Fine! I'll call him tonight. You guys go on home. And thank you so much for all your help today. It put a big dent in the work load for me."

"I wish I was handier with a hammer," said Hillary. "You sure the mud will cover those dents I put in the new gyprock?"

Emily didn't bother to glance back at the section of wall her sister had been working on. A few extra depressions in the wall board were the least of her worries. "I'm positive, sis. Besides, the lunch you brought along more than made up for your lack of finesse with hand tools. Especially the chocolate brownies you made for dessert. You'd give Caitlyn a run for the money with those." She gave Hillary then Joe a heartfelt squeeze before seeing them to the front door.

"I'll be back next week to see what I can do about your front steps." Joe took his wife by the hand and led her down the plank.

"Thanks again. I really appreciate the help."

"No problem," they replied together. "See you later."

It took all night and half the next day to work up her courage to call Ben. She decided to work on her current story in the morning, intent on polishing off *Hallowed Hikers* before heading back to Oak Boulevard.

She glared at the screen.

Nothing.

The apartment was deathly quiet. Emily went to the stereo in her bedroom and turned on a local radio station. A gentle background buzz infused the empty space in her head. She went back to her laptop and glared at the screen again, made a half-hearted attempt at some edits, then stopped to make a cup of tea. It took several minutes of rifling through the cupboard before she finally chose the Red Zinger. Maybe that would perk up her brain cells.

Nope. The half-finished tea was tepid before she threw her hands in the air and cursed out loud. Finally, it occurred to her that she'd be unable to concentrate on anything until she called him. She picked up her mobile phone.

Emily's heart beat so loud she was sure Ben could hear it pounding through the air waves. When he suggested meeting in two days her pulse quickened all the more. Ben had booked a shopping expedition in Bangor for Wednesday and would be free later that morning.

They arranged to meet at The Hungry Owl. Just the thought of seeing him made her flush – the way he looked at her, that sheepish gaze, watching her every move as she toyed with her wine glass and ate her meal. She had pretended not to notice. Maybe he hadn't held a grudge after all.

Sure, and maybe pigs would start wearing polka-dot pajamas.

Wednesday morning, Emily slept through her alarm. She'd had a fitful night, tossing and turning before sleep finally came. She glanced at the clock beside her bed. Nine a.m. Holy crap! She tossed her duvet aside and bolted to the bathroom for a quick shower.

She'd been unable to concentrate on anything besides the hunting assignment since Sunday afternoon after talking to Joe and Hillary. Or was it Ben she couldn't stop thinking about? *Get your ass in gear girl. No time to start thinking about him now.*

She rinsed off the soapy lather, dried quickly and wrapped a towel around herself before heading back to the bedroom to find clothes. With less than an hour to get ready there was no time to work on her current assignment. She would have to make time for

Hallowed Hikers later. Emily brought the icon out of her 'works in progress' folder and placed it directly on her desktop. It would be the first thing on her agenda, bright and early tomorrow morning.

Emily tugged a light, camel colored turtleneck over her head and pulled on a pair of black jeans that hugged her curves. She brushed her sleek auburn hair over her shoulders and slid a wisp of mulberry gloss on her lips. Then she dabbed a hint of brown mascara on the tips of her long lashes and stood back to assess herself in the vanity mirror. Satisfied with her appearance, she picked up her purse and left the apartment.

Caitlyn's routine had her out the door by six a.m. most mornings. Emily hoped she remembered to save her and Ben the table she asked her to reserve in the back corner. It was nestled in between a large bookcase and a long bay window that bore a ledge flaunting new and used books – an intimate space considering the clutter surrounding it.

When she stepped through the glass door of The Hungry Owl, bells chimed through to a back room. She inhaled the aroma of freshly brewed coffee. The café section of the store was small. Heavy oak tables jammed the central area leaving a narrow path to the order counter and coffee bar. Several people sat with steaming mugs, many reading books or periodicals they'd just acquired. In a moment Caitlyn appeared.

"Hey, girlfriend." She flashed a smile at Emily and passed her a mug from a shelf under the counter. "I saw your man. He passed in front of the store, like, five times! Must be awful sweet on you."

"No way," said Emily. "You don't even know what he looks like."

"Well if he acts like a nervous groom and resembles Mel Gibson, I'd say I know exactly what he looks like."

The door opened, bells chimed and both women looked to see Ben stroll into the café wearing faded jeans and a sherpa-lined jean jacket. Emily blushed and caught her breath.

Caitlyn rolled her crystal blue eyes. "Now who's nervous?" She laughed and put another mug up on the counter. "Help yourselves. I'll get a cot ready in the back room." Then she jumped out of reach to avoid being swat in the arm and disappeared through a swinging door.

Emily filled their mugs at the coffee bar and led Ben to the farthest corner of the café. "I can't tell you how much I appreciate you meeting me," she said, sliding into a painted wooden chair.

"The timing couldn't have been better," he assured her while taking his seat. "Inevitably household supplies run low and I'm forced to come into the city." He took a drink from his mug and smiled. "I wish I could make coffee this good."

Emily toyed with her own mug, caressing the rim. She took a sip and smiled back. "It's a special blend. Caitlyn came up with it herself."

"Well, how can I help you?"

So much for small talk. He probably wants to get this over with. She explained the assignment for an upcoming issue. There would be a three-week deadline and she had reservations about using him. It may take several interviews and she would need pictures as well. She pulled a Canon camera from an oversized slouch purse and set it on the table between them.

"It's not the best, but the resolution is high enough for magazine publication. It gets me by. Hillary gave it to me for my birthday." Emily grinned and put the camera back in her purse. "You probably don't have time for all this though. If I could just...."

"I have a hunting lodge full of antlers," Ben interrupted. "Would you like to take some pictures of them?"

Emily recognized the opportunity to be a rare gem. It hadn't escaped her that the man valued his privacy. She had spent much of the previous day doing research. She knew Ben owned nearly eight hundred acres of prime woodland near Wesley. With deeded access to an additional twenty-two hundred acres that included two salmon and trout streams, he was set up quite nicely – for a reclusive architect, who hunted to eat.

She also discovered that Ben was not the only Blackheart living near Wesley. An Ava Blackheart also appeared on land registration documents that she'd scanned. Emily first assumed that Ava was Ben's mother. But she may as well be a daughter or a sister. No personal information on Ben or any other Blackheart came up in her search. Perhaps she would be the first to give the world a glimpse into Benjamin Blackheart's private life. It would be a diamond moment in her career to write about him. A moment others might envy.

Emily took a deep breath, gave him her best smile. "That would be great!" She nodded her head. "I'd love to."

Ben's mobile phone rang from an inside pocket of his jacket. He checked the number then stopped to apologize before answering. "Sorry. It's my mother. I'll just be a second."

A wrinkle soon crossed his brow, he mumbled, "got it" and ended the call. Ben frowned then looked her in the eye. "Mother needs a prescription picked up in town. Her nurse didn't make it in to see her today. *She* was sick. I'd better go. You could come out to my place tomorrow morning. I'll be home for the day. Lots of wood to chop." He fished out a business card from his wallet and passed it across the table.

Emily grinned and picked up the card. "Thank you again for doing this for me. I didn't know where to go with this hunter thing. You're a lifesaver, really!"

"No, not really," Ben shot back. "See you tomorrow." A brief smile and a quick departure followed.

Chapter Six

Cool easterlies swept over Wesley in the predawn hours. Ben jabbed another log into the fire. He stood back and glimpsed above a bare mantel, at an ornate placard, the family coat-of-arms. Another gift from his father. It list to one side. Straightening the walnut frame, he felt a chill. How did that escape his attention? And when did it happen? Not something Jack could bump into.

A series of faint beeps lured him into the kitchen. He filled a mug with coffee. The scorching, hot brew taste bitter, or burnt, but it cleared his head.

He leaned into an open doorway taking stock of the pantry. One section of a white shelf held canned fruit, instant noodles and other packaged meals that Doris didn't take. The rest of her belongings he stored in the barn. A battered antique dresser, stacks of weathered books and magazines, some Indian trinkets. Nothing of value. He wondered if he should bother to pack the food as well.

Not that the wasted space presented a problem, but he respected her belongings and privacy. He would let Doris retrieve whatever she wanted before letting someone else into his home. There were no compulsions about taking Emily to the hunting lodge two miles further into the woods. Everything there came from either himself or his father. How long had it been since he'd paid the lodge a visit? Snow covered the ground. He remembered.

Ben hadn't seen or spoken to Doris King since the previous winter. Long enough. He tugged his phone from a hip pocket, tapped in once familiar numbers. After five long rings, voicemail answered. A raspy native voice came to life with instructions to leave a message after the tone.

"It's Ben. We have to talk." Click.

A hint of sun touched the horizon as he headed for the barn. A cold winter lay ahead according to the local almanac. Stacks of pine logs lain against a clapboard wall waited to be split into kindling. A chicken, roosting on the woodpile, glared at her master's approach through one pin-sized eye.

Ben glared back, shooed the reluctant bird from her perch and picked out a stout piece of wood. He balanced the log on a chopping block, picked up his axe and heaved. The seasoned pine offered no resistance. The steel blade went clean through the middle into the hardwood block. Ben yanked the blade free and picked up one of the split pieces. It took less than a minute to reduce the halves into long thin splints. He reached for another log.

Doris lingered in the back of his mind. It was only now that he realized feelings for her hadn't completely dissolved. Not romantic feelings. Ben wasn't sure if he had ever loved her – the way a man is *supposed* to love a woman. He felt he shorted her that way and had regrets, but he could offer no more. She had a right to leave.

She always went away. Working the schools and reservations, stretches three months long were not uncommon. Ben never fought with her about the out of town trips. Fights, if you could call them that, were infrequent. Most times he would handle a spat by slinging a gun over his shoulder and taking a long walk in the forest. Eventually the couple settled into a routine and cordial relationship that held no passion but knew no end. She always came back.

Then suddenly, on a cold mid-winter day, she disappeared. A stark note left on her pillow. One month later she dropped by to reclaim some clothing and a few personal items. But she didn't leave her door key.

Ben knew she kept ties with some of his family; his mother in particular and an uncle on his father's side who lived in Presque Isle. He allowed himself a fleeting smile. The small city in Aroostook County held fond memories for him as a boy. Aroostook was vast and, according to Uncle John, the most beautiful county in Maine.

Ben met Doris at a summer Pow Wow, the year after she enrolled at the University of Maine. She originally came from Eskasoni, the largest Micmac reservation in Nova Scotia. The Aroostook band of Micmacs had granted permission to join them when she was seventeen. Ben overlooked the tragic events that led to her relocation. She'd been a child after all.

He'd been captivated by her quiet grace and burning ambition. At the time, he welcomed her seductive overtones, too focused on his own career to seek a lover. Four years later, she moved in with him.

Now, she was gone – for good. But if she wasn't coming back, didn't she want something from him? Some compensation for…for what? He wasn't sure about the 'for what' part, but he figured Doris would know.

As for compensation, the land and the hunting lodge came before her, built on the sweat of his brow alone – and Tommy Rogers', his best friend. Ben had contractors build his current home. It was a prototype, designed to run completely off grid. The dwelling used seventy-five per cent less energy than standard housing and was fuelled by solar power. Though small, the project allowed him to experiment with eco-friendly products and a dozen energy-saving techniques.

Its construction consumed Ben for the most part of a year. Though she tried to hide it, Doris felt neglected and Ben could sense that. If only she had shown some interest in his work.

Tommy was also native, but again, not from Aroostook. His Micmac roots were firmly planted back in Eskasoni. Until Ben introduced them, the name Doris King meant nothing to him. He'd never been one to give rumors credence.

Unlike his friend, the thought of Doris haunted Ben. She could hurt him where it hurt the most. Would she have the land carved up, acreages sold off to cover her gambling debts?

Gambling – the one thing he knew she lied about in their near decade together. More than once she had come home broke with dubious explanations. Not that he ever needed her help financially, but she was irresponsible and that bothered him. Had there been other things to worry about, he wouldn't know.

A shrill ring broke the tempo of steel on wood. Ben snapped up his phone. A name flashed across the screen. The axe fell beside the chopping block, a glint of sun smacking off the blade.

"Tommy! What's up, brother?"

Chapter Seven

The staccato tap of a woodpecker grew loud as Emily progressed down the narrow gravel lane. Chipmunks chattered in the trees above. Song birds filled the air with chirps and whistles. The cool morning air felt wonderful when she rolled down the car window and took a deep cleansing breath. An aromatic woodland coaxed her onward.

As the lane broadened, Ben's Jeep came into view. Then the house. Emily had never seen anything like it. Solar panels covered most of one slanted roofline. From the car, it was hard to tell how many rooflines comprised the whole structure. Near the center, a cement block chimney leaned into another section of the house. Glass windows appeared to be everywhere in various shapes and sizes. A notched out section of chimney had been packed with fire logs. It took a moment to focus on Ben.

He stood near the railing on a wide veranda cradling an oversized mug, his free hand waving her in beside the Jeep. A second, steaming mug lay on a small, glass-topped table. Two rattan chairs with cushions in a paisley print were close at hand.

Emily slipped out of the car and walked trance-like towards the veranda. It was low to the ground, a single step connecting it to a river stone driveway. Emily took in Ben's tall, muscular frame and blinked away a lustful thought before meeting his gaze. Dark blue eyes sparkled like jewels in the glow of the morning sun.

"This is some pad you have here. I've never seen anything like it." She caught an amused smile and blushed. "I'm sorry, I didn't even say hello. Can I start over?"

"Hello Emily! It's so nice to see you again." His gracious tone put her at ease.

"Nice to see you again, Benjamin." She sat in the chair he motioned towards then allowed him to take her hand and bring it to his lips.

"My pleasure. You can call me Ben."

"Are you known as Gentle Ben in these parts? You're quite in the woods here aren't you?" She let her eyes roam over his rock-hard body as he took his seat and pulled over one of the steaming mugs.

"I hope you like it black. I normally have maple syrup for company who prefer it sweetened, but I'm afraid I gave too much away in the spring and left myself short. Seems to always be the way." Ben took a swig from his mug and placed it on the table.

"Black is fine," said Emily. She took a small sip, smiled politely and put down the mug. It was unequivocally the worst coffee she had ever tasted.

"No," Ben said finally. He sat back, crossed his legs and linked his fingers behind his head. "I've been called a lot of things, but to my knowledge, 'gentle' isn't one of them. I'm a hunter. I kill animals. I shoot and trap them. I share the meat of course, but I do like to harvest a variety of wild game…meat that's unadulterated by modern farm techniques and slaughterhouses."

Emily detected a hint of disgust in his last statement, but his demeanor stayed calm. "So, you're *not* a sports hunter? No trophy case, no library full of stuffed heads, no pictures of you with celebrities posing over dead animals?"

Ben leaned forward shaking his head. "No, none of that nonsense. If that's what you're writing about, I'm afraid I'm not going to be much help to you. But if you want to write about hunting, or survival, or about a people's right to feed and clothe their families…"

"A people?" Emily interrupted.

"Sorry, I meant all people. Though there's one faction I have a particular respect for."

He took a picture from his shirt pocket and passed it across the table. Ben stood among a group of First Nations youth in what looked to be a recreational hall. Long tables held a variety of sharp tools and bundles of saplings. In the photo, Ben's hands rest on the shoulders of the two tallest boys while a child in front held a longbow across his knee. The boys' faces all bore wide, white toothy smiles.

Emily flipped the photograph over. "When was this taken? You hunt with bow and arrow? No guns!"

"Well, yes, there will be guns. It's been many moons since I've gone after game with a bow and arrow. I'll tell you more once we get underway." Ben took the photo from Emily and tucked it back in his pocket.

She flushed when their fingers touched momentarily. A thin bead of sweat emerged across Ben's brow. He glanced down at the wide veranda boards. A knot in one of the planks had come loose. He nudged it with the toe of his boot.

Emily had just let the words 'get underway' formulate in her brain. Was the hunting lodge not on the same property?

"I hope your roommate is good at following directions. Thankfully, this Caitlyn person you're affiliated with knows your size requirements. You had already left by the time I called to tell you about the change of plans, so I hope you don't mind that I took the liberty of outfitting you for our trip. With mother's help of course. I didn't have time to do any last minute shopping."

"Excuse me!" Emily's head began to throb. "You never mentioned anything about a trip. I came here for pictures and an interview. I thought your hunting lodge was nearby. Have I misunderstood?"

"Not at all, but an opportunity came up early this morning to go moose hunting and we're running out of time. If we're going to make our connection, we have to leave now. I'll explain everything on the way."

Ben picked up his mug, tossed the dregs over the side of the railing and stood abruptly, expectantly, waiting for Emily's response. She sat dumbfounded, a myriad of questions whirling in her head.

"You have peed in the woods before, haven't you?" he asked with an edge of unsureness. Taking in her freshly polished pink fingertips he continued. "I'm afraid permanent lavatory service is unavailable in the Highlands. But I have taken care and preparations to make your stay as comfortable as possible considering the short notice."

"Well, yes, of course...when I camped as a child with my family. But what does that...who are we supposed...how can I?" Failing to utter a coherent sentence, Emily rose from her seat shaking her head not knowing what to do next.

Ben said nothing for several seconds, then opened his palm and reached for her hand. "Emily Paige, do you want a story...or do you *want* a story?"

Emily looked past the veranda to where the Jeep sat parked. The back of the vehicle appeared to be packed to the roof with duffle bags and rubber totes. Both front seats were empty.

Emily desperately wanted this story – his story. To what extreme she wasn't sure. "What's the worst that could happen?" She hadn't meant to voice her thoughts.

His pleading eyes tugged once more, then she took his hand.

"One more thing…you aren't afraid to fly are you?"

Emily abandoned her Colt and they left within moments in the over-stuffed Jeep. She took a notebook from her slouch purse. Ben grinned and turned down the stereo. Jimmy Buffet faded into the background and Emily settled back into her seat. She opened the notebook. There were so many questions, so much to learn. Research produced little information.

Ben appeared in numerous stories in keeping with Blackheart Designs. But these were mere endorsements of the work. Most of his projects garnered publicity. They were unique, conservational and coveted.

Benjamin Blackheart could afford to be eccentric. Off radar. But was he completely off grid? Emily noted a power line on his private road, on the laneway leading up to his odd shaped dwelling and beyond. He was remote, but not without the amenities of a modern twenty-first century home. So she thought.

Further questioning revealed that the power poles went to Ava's property. Ben's home produced its own power. Heat came from an endless supply of hardwood.

"Harvesting wood is a constant chore, but it keeps me in shape and out of trouble."

Emily gave him a questioning look. "Trouble?"

"The devil makes work of idle hands. That's a notion favored by my mother."

Ben's smile at the mention of Ava told Emily that they were close. "And, do you also take care of your mom?" Emily knew the question was personal, out of line even, considering the nature of her visit. But she was curious.

"Yes, since my father passed away last spring. I'm all she has left. Her lone wolf," he said and grinned. "She's pretty independent though. I'm more indispensable in the winter when the roads have to be plowed and her porch and steps need to be cleared of snow and ice. She'll be seventy six this year. My biggest fear is that she'll fall and break a bone. She still drives."

"Oh dear. I can imagine how worrisome that would be. Is there more?"

"Well, there's the vegetables and fruit trees behind my place." His tone changed when he brought up the orchards and gardening. "Sadly neglected this year. The rains this spring were endless. Everything struggled." He pulled onto the main highway and picked up speed.

"Now lately, the weather has vastly improved. The whole weekend is supposed to be clear and sunny. Cooler, but that's a good thing. If we get lucky right away, the cold will help to keep the meat fresh."

They spent the rest of the hour-long drive to Bangor and a private airfield trading childhood memories and family stories. Emily learned that Ben had come from a long line of Scottish descendants whose lineage dated back to a time when an armada of sailing ships, the 'white sails', plied the stormy Atlantic Ocean. The Scots of that era called them the coffin ships. Emily admitted she hadn't explored her family tree, though she believed all her ancestors to be of European descent.

She told him about Hillary's parental instincts bursting forth after their parents were killed in a traffic accident. She was eighteen, in her last year of high school, when tragedy struck. While other girls and boys were thinking about year-end celebrations, prom dresses and parties, Emily knew only grief and pain. Dark thoughts consumed her from morning until night when she cried herself to sleep.

There would be no thinking about parties or boys. She had to help Hillary pick out clothing; a light, floral print dress for her mother, her father's favorite grey, pinstriped suit. She helped to pack the rest of her parents clothing in bags to give to the Veteran's charity. Emily learned that Ben's father also served overseas in the Second World War. They may even had trod African soil together, though neither Ben nor Emily could draw on details.

They grew quiet as Ben veered off the highway and picked up a road with grass and weeds growing through deep cracks in the pavement. They drove through the private airfield and pulled up beside a taxi parked beside a blue and white twin-engine Maule.

"You have your own airplane? Who's the pilot?" Emily's pulse twitched. She scanned the field. Of the few people milling around, none came towards them.

"Well, yes, it is mine." Ben lowered his eyes. "Actually it belongs to my company. I'm the pilot, a military brat. Learned to fly in air cadets many moons ago."

They left the truck and Ben went to speak with the cab driver. He took some bills from his wallet and passed them through a window. Then he opened the back door to extract a small, green Safari suitcase. The taxi drove away.

"Is that mine?" Emily recognized the case immediately.

"It is." Ben packed the case and the rest of the gear from the Jeep into the airplane. Then Emily followed him, still dumbfounded, to the passenger side of the Maule. "Hop in!"

Emily shook her head. "I've never been in anything this small."

"No worries. The weather report forecasts clear skies, light winds and calm seas. We'll be there before you know it," said Ben.

His enthusiasm was contagious but wariness tugged at Emily's conscience. "I should call my sister. She'll be worried if she doesn't hear from me."

Ben came around and jumped in the pilot's seat beside her. "She already knows. I called this morning to make sure you didn't have any drug requirements or allergies I should know about. Apparently you're healthy as a horse." He grinned when Emily punched his arm not so lightly.

"Yes, well I'd like to keep it that way. Fly carefully please." She didn't know what else to say.

Ben checked in with a crackling voice on his headset, turning knobs and flipping switches as he listened and acknowledged instructions. He checked Emily's seatbelt, for the third time, and gave her the drill on emergency landings. That took less than a minute. Then they taxied down a rough asphalt runway and scooted into the late morning sky.

The three hour flight to Debert, and an even smaller airfield in central Nova Scotia, went by without incident. Emily spent much of the time trying to take pictures out the small triangular shaped window in the door beside her. She marveled at the sights below and tingled at the prospect of seeing wildlife in its natural surroundings. Once they reached their peak altitude at thirty-five hundred feet she put her camera away and took the notebook out of her purse.

"How's this for virtual reality?" said Ben. "Beats any computer generated game I've ever tried."

"Somehow I find it hard to picture you doing anything of the sort," Emily said. "You didn't get to where you are today playing video games I'm sure."

"No, but kids today spend a lot of time on them don't they. If given the opportunity I'm sure most would prefer to do what I now take for granted. I was lucky."

Emily did most of the talking over the next few hours. She was wary of anything going amiss, though she had no idea how she would recognize a problem should one arise. Talking calmed her nerves.

Have faith, she told herself. Ben knows what he's doing. She recounted the events leading up to her landing a job at Outdoor American and told him she hoped to keep renovating and flipping houses on the side. When he asked about boyfriends she shook her head and frowned.

"I've had plenty of dates. None that turned into anything serious. Most of the guys I meet are either jerks, just looking to get laid, or married...or gay. I guess I haven't had much luck with men."

Ben took everything in, interrupting on occasion to point out a formation of geese heading south and anything scenic of note.

They'd flown over coastal Nova Scotia and were nearing their destination by the time she finished telling him about her disappointing love life.

A noisy crackling came in through Ben's headset. He responded and pointed to a landing strip that looked ominously short to Emily. "We're going down!"

"Weeee!" said Emily. She tried to sound enthusiastic, but her stomach churned inside as the airplane noticeably slowed and dropped out of the sky. She was relieved when Ben brought the airplane to a complete stop just before the runway ended.

He waited a minute, scanning the airstrip for pedestrian activity, then taxied over to a Ford half-ton sporting Maine license plates parked beside a small hangar. Ben jumped out and came around to help Emily out of the Maule. They transferred the gear and climbed into the truck. Its gun-steel grey exterior and chunky near-new tires were crusted in mud. Within moments they were buckled up and on their way to the Cape Breton Highlands.

The sky stayed clear, the air warm, until they reached the base of the mountain range. According to the Ben, this remote part of Nova Scotia was renowned for its scenic beauty and infamous for its unpredictable weather. When they stopped to stretch their legs and buy apples and ready-made sandwiches at a small market along the way, Emily put on the fall jacket she'd brought with her on the way to Ben's that morning.

"Will it get very cold where we're going?" she asked.

"Freezing cold," said Ben smiling. "Don't worry, there will be lots to do to keep you warm. How are you at chopping wood?"

"I'm not," said Emily. "At least I've never had to do it, so I'm not quite sure. Maybe I'm a natural." She bit into an apple and moaned with delight. "I love honey crisp!" She wiped a dribble of juice from her chin with the back of her hand.

She gasped when Ben grabbed her fingers and kissed the juice away before spinning her towards the truck. She sashayed across the parking lot.

Soon they were on their way again, the narrow highway snaking through small villages and reservations with names that were, to Emily, nothing short of exotic. Houses were small, pale wooden structures with few embellishments. Simple church steeples stood tall and thin against the empty skyline. The sun fell behind them as they drove through Whycocomagh, a Micmac reservation. They turned left off highway 105 onto an older route that led to a series of dirt roads that ended in no-man's land – moose country.

Cushioning the narrow roads, birch, maple and poplar brazenly flashed a spectacular collage of fall colors. High above the dappled border of red, copper and gold loomed a swath of dark green forest crisscrossed with thin brown lines and patches of clear cut. The blue sky appeared as deep and as vast as an ocean.

"What a beautiful day. We really couldn't ask for better," said Ben.

"Postcard perfect," replied Emily. Spotting eagles in the distance she took out her camera and set it between them to have on hand in case they came closer.

"It won't be long now. Would you like to listen to some music? Radio reception is lost from here." Ben opened a console between the two seats and showed her a collection of CDs, mostly light rock, a little folk music, some blue grass.

"Actually I'd like to ask you some questions," said Emily.

She opened her slouch purse again and pulled out her notebook. The purse held many of her personal items: a wallet and ID, brush and hair elastics, some nail and dental supplies, as well as lip gloss and hand cream. Enough to get her through the whole weekend. She wondered what Caitlyn had packed for her from home. Then it hit her. Home. Where she should be right now. Sweet anticipation coupled with a seething angst jarred her nerves.

Emily couldn't believe she was in Canada for the weekend with Ben – a world away – yet surprisingly close to home. She hadn't imagined getting there so soon either, given conventional travel. Then again, Ben didn't seem to hold much for convention. He was a different sort for sure. He was also quiet and reflective, giving little away unless asked directly.

Getting him to open up may take more work than she'd anticipated. Some people made bad interview subjects no matter how specialized their talent. She noticed that he barely talked about the expedition, his friends, their sleeping arrangements. Suddenly, this once-in-a-lifetime trip filled her with a bliss she couldn't name and a panic she knew too well.

Chapter Eight

Nothing could be done with the hiker story until Sunday night or Monday morning. Not much to do really. Some final edits. Emily determined to polish it up when she returned. At the moment, all she wanted to think about was Ben.

"You haven't said much about your friends. Tell me about them. How did you meet?" Ben was forthcoming with an answer. Though, by the way he kept veering off course she assumed that he was giving her the short version of a much longer tale. She urged him to keep talking – his previous stories being vivid and not without humor.

"I can't wait for you to meet them. You'll love Tommy and Michelle," he said finally. "They're straight up people. Just watch out for the jokester, Tommy. He'll do anything for a laugh."

Emily gave up the drill and began to take in the rise of elevation and the changing landscape. As they wound their way through rural Cape Breton on their way to the Highlands, clouds of dust billowed behind them. Three trucks passed them coming down the mountain. Each one had moose heads with antlers trussed up to their tailgates.

Emily noticed that the drivers were all native men. No women travelled with them. Ben explained that only band members could harvest moose without a license. The hunting season for the general population opened the coming weekend. Then, those lucky enough to get a draw would be able to hunt legally.

They climbed for almost an hour before coming to an unmarked intersection and turning onto another dry dirt road. Emily held onto the dash as they bounced across a makeshift bridge made of logs. It looked as though it had been built in the last century. A thin creek flowed beneath into a pool of blackish water and continued toward an expanse of land swaddled in a blanket of low growing shrubbery.

"I'll have to ask you to stay close to camp when we get there. If you wander away you could get stuck in a killer bog and swallowed up," said Ben.

Emily grinned, not sure if he was toying with her. She looked into his eyes for a glimmer of humor, but a stern look told her he was serious. "I thought all I had to worry about was bull moose and black bears," she said. "You didn't tell me about the killer bogs."

"I'm telling you now. There are coyotes too. Don't stray too far from camp."

Emily sat back in her seat and rolled her window down. Four bald eagles soared in a tight circle overhead. "They're magnificent," said Emily. "Are they endangered here?"

"I don't think so," said Ben. "Keep your eyes peeled. You may even see a golden. That would be rare, but I hear they've been spotted a couple of times in the last few years."

Emily cast her gaze out the window again. A thin wisp of cloud trailed across the endless sky. The eagles had flown out of sight. Too late to snap a picture.

A moment later Ben pulled off the road onto a narrow trail overgrown with coarse grass and lined with long shards of yarrow. The puffy white and yellow heads were a welcome splash of color against the backdrop of greens and browns that pervaded the landscape. A minute later the lane widened and became a flat round patch of dirt and gravel backing into a curve of balsam trees. A variety of mosses hunkered low over shallow roots and engulfed the outskirts of the clearing.

Tire tracks leading in stopped at a white tent trailer. Two camp chairs sat under a canvas awning that swayed on thin aluminum poles. It appeared that Tommy and Michelle had set up and left to do some scouting.

"They should be back soon," said Ben.

He passed the trailer and pulled in beside a decrepit looking fifth wheel slumped over to the right side of the clearing. "I know it's not the Ritz, but for hunters and mountain men, it does the trick. Let's go inside and see how bad it is. I asked Tommy to bring a new three-man tent, just for you, if you find it too rugged to sleep in."

Emily gaped at the wasting slabs of plywood and rust-stained metal, a vague image forming of what it must look like inside. She sucked in her breath as Ben leaned over and undid her seat belt, then reached across to open her door.

"Well, I'd prefer not to sleep in a tent outside by myself. It's such nice weather...we probably won't be spending too much time inside."

Emily had no intention of spending the weekend cleaning up camp for a bunch of hunters. Not that *any* of this was her intention. She still hadn't completely shaken off the feeling that she'd been hit with a stun gun. Here she was in the middle of nowhere surrounded by mountain men, guns and wild animals. No, this was not her intention at all.

Ben went to the open door of the camper and looked in. Then he came back to the truck, undid the tailgate and grabbed the duffle bags. Emily tested the weight of the rubber totes, found one that she could easily manage and followed him inside.

"Michelle must have opened the door and windows to air it out for us. We'll have to thank her," he said.

A thin rawhide strip indeed had been looped around the doorknob and hooked over a peg on an inside wall. A large blackfly zoomed past Emily's head and flew outside. She looked in the direction it came from and noticed a pan of enamel dishes with bits of dried egg and toast crumbs on them.

"Smells like musty bacon and eggs," said Emily. "I take it your friends were here for breakfast."

Ben nodded. "It won't take long to air out, considering it's been closed up for the best part of a year. You'll notice a big difference once the fire is going."

Emily set the rubber tote down on the floor and looked around. She was pleasantly surprised with her weekend accommodations. The rough façade hid a room built out from the back side of the trailer. It added a further eight feet to the space and was fabricated from an assortment of plywood slabs and reclaimed glass. A crusty black woodstove stood to the side on a sheet of thin steel. Its pipe shot up through a hole in the ceiling. Beside the stove sat a box full of dry weathered newspapers, some cardboard and long splints of pine. There were two bunks on opposite sides of the add-on, one under an open window.

"Would you like the window or the dark side?" Ben asked, ready to drop her bag on any preference she might have. "I can sleep outside in the tent if you need more privacy," he added with reluctance.

Emily pointed to the dark side. "I think I'd sleep better knowing a bear couldn't crawl in the window and eat me. I'm sure I'd worry less if you were inside as well. You know, for protection."

Ben put a duffle bag on Emily's bunk and set another on the floor beside the window.

"You'd still have to worry about the bear."

"What do you mean? You wouldn't kill it to save our lives?"

"No. I told you, I'd never shoot an animal I didn't intend to eat. Besides, all I'd have to do is run. As long as I can run faster than you, I have nothing to worry about." His laughter cut through the somber atmosphere.

Emily snatched the bare pillow from her bunk and aimed for Ben's head, but he jumped back and let the pillow slap his arm instead. Then he caught hers and pulled her towards him crushing her to his chest.

"Emily, I swear...nothing bad will happen to you. You have my word. Besides, Hillary would kill me. Am I right?"

Emily nodded and peered into somber pools of promise. She closed her eyes and tilted her head towards his lips. Ben suddenly stepped back and let go of Emily's arm.

"Yes, right. Absolutely." She whirled around to her bunk and gestured at the duffle bag. "Can I open it now?"

"Of course, here let me show you."

Ben was glad to see her quick recovery. He still reeled from her perfume, from their near kiss. What was he thinking? He had intended to be a gentleman when he asked Emily to come on the impromptu hunting trip. In truth, he didn't believe she would come. Everything happened so fast. She surprised him at every turn. And now she wanted him to sleep in the same room with her. He would have to be careful.

He unzipped the duffle bag and Emily leaned over to have a peek. He reached in and brought out a full set of thermal underwear in a pink floral. It was brand new, still wrapped in plastic. Next he pulled out a thick woolen car coat, dark green and navy plaid. A full set of rain gear appeared next. There were wool sweaters and thick wool socks as well.

A separate bag in the bottom held two sets of footwear. He took out a pair of green rubber boots with heavy felt liners and a pair of moccasins, dark brown cowhide, trimmed with a short suede fringe. Colored beads in the shape of an eagle were stitched into the top. They were lined with soft fur and the soles were rawhide rubbed smooth. He glanced down at her feet, which were clad in light, leather walking shoes. Not so appropriate for wilderness terrain.

"These are lovely," said Emily stroking the soft fur inside the slippers. "Everything. It must have cost a small…"

Ben put his index finger to her lips and stopped her midsentence.

"Mother supplied the warm clothing. She said you can keep anything you like. And it isn't that much really, so don't worry. You don't have to pay her back and if you don't want any of this after the weekend, I'll donate it to charity. No ties. Okay?"

"If you say so." Emily was relieved and suddenly aware of growling noises coming from her stomach. "I'm starved. Should we go out and bag some dinner or did your friends bring all the food? I noticed we didn't stop for much on the way."

"Well, we could go fishing!"

Emily shot him a warning glance. "I thought Tommy was supposed to be the jokester."

Ben chuckled and went back to the truck to get another tote on the tailgate. When he lifted the lid, it revealed a cooler and several cloth shopping bags. Inside was a smorgasbord of market fresh pastries and breads, fresh fruit, cheeses and eggs.

"The eggs are compliments of my ladies – my Bantams that is. I have a dozen egg producing chickens. I lost the rooster last week…to a weasel I'm pretty sure. I hope he doesn't bother the hens. They don't need a rooster to lay, but he was part of the family. I even miss his annoying crow in the morning. Damn thing used to start squawking two hours before sunup. I almost shot him myself a couple of times." He winked at Emily and grinned.

Then he sliced down on a piece of aged white cheddar with a pocketknife he unsheathed from a leather case on his belt. Emily found a breadknife in a drawer on the kitchen side of the trailer and sawed off four hunks of fresh multigrain bread. Ben produced a plastic butter dish and guided Emily to a table that stuck out between two padded bench seats.

"Sit," he commanded, a playful smile crossing his lips. He placed the dish on the table and took a bag of paper plates from the tote Emily brought in. He put the bread and cheese on plates and brought them to the table. "You get to do the dishes." He grinned and sat down.

"I'd love to," she replied.

Tommy and Michelle had yet to appear after they ate, so Ben suggested they do some scouting on their own. Maybe bring back some more firewood. They would definitely need water. One of the larger totes contained fresh bed linens and quilts. He set these on the bunks then put the empty tote in the back of the truck.

Emily took the paper plates from the table and shook the crumbs off outside the still open door. She had seen whiskey jacks flitting about in the trees nearby and didn't think they could resist the tempting morsels. "These could go a second round," she said. "Waste not want not." She set the paper plates back on the table before strutting back to the truck sporting her nearly new rubber boots.

"As long as you're not shirking your duties," said Ben

Emily looked back and rolled her eyes, but she didn't respond. He followed behind, admiring the view, then darted ahead to open her door. It took only a minute to amble down the narrow lane and reach the main road.

Ben tore down the hard packed earth leaving clouds of dust in their wake. They sped past the barrens and found themselves delving deep into a forest where the road became a series of long ruts with sections deeply gouged by heavy rains. Some still held slick muddy water despite the present state of aridness.

Up ahead, a mud splattered truck wobbled towards them slow and steady. When it reached them, the man inside stopped and rolled down his window. "Got smoke." His gruff voice was expectant. He peered across Ben to get a better look at Emily.

"No, no smoke," said Ben. "Sorry...she's pregnant." He grimaced and patted Emily's knee, like a concerned husband. The excuse seemed to suit the dark skinned man. He huffed, rolled up his window and wobbled on.

Emily realized that Ben, who looked much younger than his years, wore his fifty shades of grey hair on the long side. It grazed the back of his collar and a thick bang slashed across his brow giving him a rakish look. Bronzed from the summer sun he could easily be mistaken for at least part native – or a latent Yankee hippy. Emily remembered they were riding Maine plates.

"Okay, now why did you tell him I was pregnant? I don't even have a boyfriend. You know that." Emily was a little miffed. It felt like she was missing the joke even though she was glad to have the opportunity to remind him of her status. She wondered if he cared.

Ben laughed. "Ricky? Maybe I didn't tell you. I've been coming up here for years. Bound to recognize some of the locals. Sometimes a white lie is needed to ensure privacy though. He'll tell the rest of his camp and they'll leave us alone. I respect their culture, but I only indulge in what suits me. Drugs and alcohol don't mix well with hunting. Not everyone up here agrees unfortunately, so I try not to let my guard down. You'd be wise to do the same."

The road flattened out then ended abruptly. A spring ran into a pond directly ahead of them. From the slick and trodden down embankment surrounding it, Emily guessed it to be a popular watering hole for man and beast alike.

Ben got out and took the empty tote down to the water, filling it from the spring. She watched from the truck as he put the lid on and attempted to carry it back up the slick incline. The tote, now heavy and sloshing inside, knocked him off balance. He slipped and fell backwards with a splat. The lid bounced off from the impact of gushing water and the torrent splashed over him.

Emily leapt from the truck and ran to the edge of the bank, her heart in her throat. Seeing Ben sitting in the mud dripping wet, a shocked expression on his face, she couldn't stop herself. It was too funny. She doubled over in laughter.

"Are you okay?" She asked, stifling a final giggle. "Can I give you a hand?"

Ben scowled and began to extract himself from the mud but was sucked back down. He underestimated the weight of his woolen jacket. Icy cold water now saturated the fibers.

Emily held her breath to keep from laughing again. Ben unbuttoned himself and pulled his arms free. Then he stood up and yanked his coat out of the mud. Emily expected to hear a tirade of curses spring from the hapless man, but Ben maintained his stony silence. He simply shook his head in wonder, avoiding Emily's now sympathetic stare. She clambered down the bank taking the driest route she could find and retrieved the rubber tote that he'd managed to fling into a wall of cattails.

Ben was up on the road by the time she came around to where the spring emptied into the pond. She filled the tote and put the lid on tight before dragging it back to the base of the incline. There was no way she could lift it.

Ben had changed into a dry sweatshirt that he'd kept behind his seat in the truck, though his face and hair were still wet and splattered with mud. There was nothing he could do about his wet jeans, for the moment. He eased his way down to Emily and together they lugged the swilling tote up the bank and onto the back of the truck. Ben snapped the tailgate shut. Then he jumped in the truck and started the motor.

Emily could no longer stand the silence. "Are you alright?" she asked, gently closing her door.

Ben glared at her. He quavered for several seconds, then stilled. "Sorry. I'm fine. Just cold and wet. Let's get back to camp." He patted her knee, turned the truck around and turned on the headlights. It would soon be dark. They headed back over the twisted road. Emily leaned forward and cranked on the heater.

The soft glow of a campfire emanated from the clearing when Ben turned down the narrow lane. Tommy and Michelle were in their camp chairs roasting wieners amid hot wooden coals. A mixture of birch and maple logs lay roughly stacked between their trailers near the tree-line. Ben backed in beside their temporary quarters and they got out. He led Emily over to the fire to meet his friends.

Once introductions were out of the way, Tommy looked at Ben and said, "Holy hell! Bit late in the year for swimming. Did you forget to take off your pants? Come on Michelle, let's go show them how to swim eh? Take off your drawers."

"Bugger off, Tommy. Can't you see Ben has a guest here? Mind yourself will you!" Michelle was stern but not mean at all.

Emily could tell that Tommy was being playful and his girlfriend was trying to be nice. "That's okay, I'm not really here for the swimming," she said. "I'm writing an article about hunting for the magazine I work for. Ben was kind enough to ask me to come along. So far it's been quite the experience."

"Great, well you guys get acquainted while I go change out of these wet jeans," said Ben. He had brought two more camp chairs out of the back of his half-ton and set them close to the fire. He guided Emily to one of the seats before he left to change.

"How you liking the Ritz?" asked Tommy. "We been calling it that since I dragged it up here five years ago. It was stolen you know?"

"No, I didn't know," admitted Emily. "Did you steal it?"

"No," said Tommy. "Well...not the first time."

Michelle chuckled, but she didn't add anything. Emily assumed she'd heard this story many times before.

"The pair of Indians who originally took it, from a deserving bloke in Bible Hill, got to the causeway going to Cape Breton. Then they had to pull off the road for the night. They'd been drunk from the time they hitched the trailer onto one of their trucks. Me and Ricky saw the pair right from the start and followed them. As soon as we knew they were passed out, we unhitched their pickup and hitched ours unto it instead. Then we brought her up here to make a camp. Works pretty good don't she?"

Michelle was laughing now. "He gave it to me so I'd come on hunts with him, but I wouldn't have nothing to do with it. Stolen is stolen, and I don't agree with what they'd done. Not one bit," she added emphatically.

"Go 'way, you nit!" said Tommy, chomping into a charred wiener. "You slept in it that once, when you first agreed to come up here with us."

"Yes, once. And, only once. They scared me half to death, Tommy, Ricky and Ben. Em, my darling, come closer so I can tell you what happened."

Emily pulled her chair closer and listened as Michelle recounted waking up in the morning to the sound of a chainsaw cutting through board and metal. The men decided the trailer was too cramped. They were literally on top of each other, so it had to be renovated.

"Didn't even wait for me to get my skivvies on, the dogs. They just ripped the back wall off and started nailing on the new plywood. I could have shot the works of them. I know how to shoot too you know?"

"I didn't know," said Emily.

"Believe her. She's one hell of a sharpshooter," said Ben coming up behind them in a pair of dry sweatpants. "Much better than Tommy I'd say."

Michelle looked up in dismay. "Don't say such foolishness, Ben. You know my Tommy is the best shooter in all Cape Breton. He could take down a calf moose from three hundred yards and not miss his mark. You know that."

She huffed and grabbed the bag of wieners at her feet. She offered a round but had no takers, so she put them down again.

"Now honey, you know we don't like to harvest calves out from under their mothers," Tommy said. "They're some tasty though aren't they, Ben?" He laughed and made some smacking noises with his lips before unleashing a series of moans.

A picture of a baby moose came to Emily's mind and she hoped Tommy was joking. There was no way to tell for sure. She glanced over at the Ritz. Ben had started a fire inside, making it look more and more inviting.

"Well, I think I'll turn in then. I'm bushed already with all this fresh air."

Ben rose from his chair to follow, but Emily stopped him.

"I'll find everything I need. You stay with your friends. I'm just too tired to stay up any longer." She leaned into him and finished in a whisper, "and tell them all about me. I know they're curious."

She said goodnight to Tommy and Michelle, then left them with Ben to hear *his* side of the story.

A wall of heat met Emily when she opened the metal camp door and went inside. The musty odor was mostly gone, replaced by the smell of burning wood and Ivory soap. Ben left a kerosene lantern burning on the table. It cast a flickering glow that softened the starkness and did well to hide the grime in their squalid accommodations.

His damp jeans were draped over a metal folding chair beside the woodstove. The dirty dishes had disappeared. A pan of grey water with a few lingering bubbles lay in the sink where Ben washed up.

Emily took off her boots and the heavy wool jacket Ben brought for her. She slipped on the pretty moccasins, went to her bunk and yawned. She didn't feel like cleaning up. She needed sleep. Every bone in her body told her so.

Four inch slabs of grungy yellow foam covered the double wide bunks. At the foot of each, Ben had placed a pile of bedding. She made both beds, thankful that the sheets were thick flannel. She didn't think they were freshly laundered, but they were clean and warm.

The quilts were homemade and heavier than they looked. One had a pattern of interlocking colored rings over beige. Another was traditional, sewn of small squares and triangles in colors and fabrics too numerous to count. The underside was a solid baby blue. Emily chose the patchwork quilt for herself and made Ben's bed with the beige one.

She still hadn't opened the Safari suitcase that Caitlyn prepared for her. She hoped to find her long sleeved pajamas inside. Then she remembered that Ben told her what to pack. Emily put the case up on her bunk and opened it, not sure what to expect.

A light tapping noise stopped her from exploring further. It took her a moment to realize it was coming from the door. "Come in," she called out. "It's not locked."

Ben entered sheepishly and took in the bunks freshly made. He looked tired. "Michelle and Tommy wanted to go to bed too. I guess we all had an early start this morning and it's been a long day. How are you doing?"

"I was just looking for something to wear to bed," said Emily. She yawned and stretched.

"I'm not sure what's in your suitcase," said Ben. "I thought you'd be more comfortable in your own underwear though. I asked your roommate to pack some old jeans if you had any, a couple of T-shirts. You don't want to bring good clothes out here in the bush. You get dirty real fast. You'll see."

"All I want to see right now is a pair of pajamas and I'm not seeing the ones I hoped Caitlyn would send, so I think I'll put on the long underwear you brought me." She took the duffle bag out from underneath her bunk and reached inside for the floral print long johns.

"Good idea," said Ben. "It's nice and warm here now with the fire going. It'll be much colder when you wake up in the morning. Which reminds me...I need something in the truck. I'll give you time to change."

"Thanks," said Emily.

Ben went outside closing the door behind him. Emily quickly stripped and put on the long underwear. They bunched around her ankles and the sleeves were too long as well, but they were warm and serviceable, unlike the slinky satin negligee that Caitlyn had packed. What was *she* thinking? Emily blushed.

A few minutes later, Ben tapped on the door and came in not waiting to be told. Emily tucked the duffle bag and the suitcase under her bunk then slipped between the sheets. She curled in and scrunched the bedding up to her chin. She contemplated turning her back to Ben's bunk but felt too tired to accomplish a shift in position so she closed her eyes instead.

She listened as he sat on the bench seat by the table and took off his boots. He padded over to the woodstove and cranked the door open, tossed in a piece of hardwood and closed the door tight. The crackling inside grew louder and drowned out the sounds of him pulling the sweatshirt over his head and crawling into the bunk wearing only his sweatpants.

"Good night," he whispered, gazing at puckered lips and the mass of auburn hair tumbling over her pillow.

There was no response. The woman he'd stolen off with that morning had already fallen into a deep slumber.

Chapter Nine

Doris King admired her slim, stark reflection in the patio glass door. She kept her hair short and dyed the deepest black to highlight her Indian features – black piercing eyes, sharp facial lines, high cheek bones. The only thing Doris didn't like about herself was her lips. Thin and unshapely, they served her well in one manner only – her vocation in counselling. She travelled the countryside giving seminars on drugs, contraband and suicide prevention. Her lips never stopped once engaged in her calling. She earned a six figure income. They served her well.

Doris wasn't thinking about her lips or money when she stamped out her cigarette. As she watched the last trails of smoke disappear into the still night air on her hotel balcony, all she could think about was Benjamin Blackheart and the curt message he left her that morning.

She'd been toying with the idea of going back to him. Winter approached and she missed the isolation and warm camaraderie they shared. When she called Ava earlier that day, the old lady had been vague in explaining Ben's sudden departure and not being able to reach him. He left to go hunting with Tommy and Michelle. She got that. Except that Tommy never took Michelle hunting. Was there a fourth party? A reporter – some Emily woman. Ben didn't give interviews. He valued his privacy too much. Perhaps it was time to go home.

She stayed up late the previous night, playing slots in the hotel casino. The grand amusement center was nearly empty, giving her the seclusion she longed for and the excitement she craved. Ben didn't share her obsession with gambling. It was his love of solitude and natural environments that intrigued her, that kept her coming back to him time after time.

The thought of Ben in a relationship left her chilled. No one she'd talked to in the last nine months mentioned other women. Certainly, no one had mentioned Emily, but she was now determined to find out more about her. When it came to Ben, she wasn't going to leave anything to chance. It was time to pack her bags.

Doris had always been bright. By two she spoke English as well as Micmac fluently and, to the chagrin of her family, non-stop if the mood struck her.

"Go watch cartoons girl," her mother would say, her throat dry from answering a barrage of questions. "I'm going to have my tea." Catching her son help himself to a handful of oatmeal cookies from a clay crock on the counter, she added, "You can have a cookie before supper if you're good."

Doris always got her cookie. She was obedient, sweet and kind. Michael was six years older, and had no shortage of friends. Some good, some bad. The good ones hung mostly at the ball field. The others lured him into places on the reserve that the Elders would not approve of. Michael was doing well in school though and had shown an interest in higher education.

He said he wanted to be a teacher like his great-grandmother, Myra King. Doris often heard her mother praying for him at night. She prayed that he would make good choices.

Doris, until the age of nine, chose to be a warrior princess. She had grown up thus far adoring princess heroines – Pocahontas in Disney, Princess Leah in *Star Wars*, Moonchild in *The Neverending Story* – there were all different types of princesses she knew, but she was the Indian princess. Even her name was royal – King!

She knew Mike wasn't happy about having to babysit his little sister while their parents drove to Sydney to buy Christmas presents. It was only the promise of an early gift that finally made him relent.

"And, you'll pay me to stay home with her?" he stammered, as they were putting on their overcoats and boots.

"Well, I guess you need some dough for Christmas too eh," said his father. He flipped a crumpled twenty out of the front pocket of his trousers and tossed it on the kitchen table. "Help yourself to the pop and chips. They're stashed in a cupboard over the refrigerator. And share with princess."

Warren King patted Doris on the head, winked at his son and went through the door nudging his wife ahead of him. A few ominous flakes of snow had begun to fall. He wanted to get this trip over with before they were caught in a storm, though none was forecast.

What brewed inside the reserve on that particular night belied the twinkling stars above and the soft glow of Christmas lights hanging from the eaves. This storm would blow in without warning. This one would leave scars and have consequences far removed from those that left people cold and without power – storms that held people captive in their homes waiting for the snow plows to arrive.

The memory of those terrible blizzards faded quickly when the promise of spring brought back the singing robins and the babbling brooks. Not this time. It would be many years before the memory of this storm melted into oblivion, and its consequences would be far more dire than any before it.

Six o'clock and Doris had just turned off the cartoons when the doorbell rang. Mike shooed her to her room, then went to let in his friends. She knew that Gunner and Vincent had come to get him. She wasn't expecting the case of beer that Gunner thrust into her brother's hand when he opened the back door. She slipped into her parent's bedroom where she could see and hear what was going on without being detected.

"I can't go out tonight guys," said Mike. "I told you. I have to babysit my sister."

"No problem. We can stay here and drink for a while. We'll be gone before your folks get back. You know they'll be away for hours."

"Sorry guys but I'm tapped. I couldn't even get enough money for the beer. You guys go on and have fun. I'll join you another time, alright?" Mike had resigned himself to staying home and out of trouble.

He had even taken out his social studies book and started on a school assignment. It was due in two weeks, just before school broke for the holidays. His book lay open on the table next to the crumpled twenty dollar bill.

"This will do," said Vincent, grabbing the bill and stuffing it in his coat pocket.

Mike started to protest but Vincent was big for his age and quickly pushed his friend down in one of the chrome legged kitchen chairs. The legs skid on the linoleum clad floor and Mike's head banged back into the wall.

"What? Don't be such a pussy!" said Vincent. "No harm in having a couple of beers. Gunner, pass us a couple will ya."

Gunner took three beer bottles out of the case, flipped the lids off with a disposable lighter and sat down. Vincent sat as well and they all took a long pull on their beers.

"There, that's better," said Vincent. He reached over and closed the text book on the table shoving it aside. "Where are the cards Mike? We should have a game."

Doris sat up on her bed, a porcupine quill in hand, studying the present she was making for her parents. She'd been crafting a box with quills on birch bark in a simple geometric pattern. Her tools and materials were gathered around her on the bed.

She usually kept to herself when Mike's friends came around. They were older boys, bigger than Mike and they reeked of stale smoke. Doris hated the smell. Mike was growing up too, but at least he smelled good, like her father. She didn't know when he started, but of late she noticed that he came out of the bathroom in the morning smelling of mint, the fragrance of her father's shaving gel.

She heard a loud bang, from the other side of her room in the kitchen and it piqued her curiosity. She thought to take another peek, just to make sure her brother was okay.

"What are you looking at little missy?" Vincent said. He caught her gaze and held on.

Mike dropped an ace on the table and looked over at Vincent, then at Doris. "Go back to your room, princess."

"I heard a noise," said Doris. Her eyes darted around the kitchen, trying to take in all that was going on.

Mike sighed heavily. "Go on now. Be a good girl."

Doris turned and went back to her bedroom. She didn't like the way that Gunner had looked at her without saying a word. She was suddenly feeling uneasy about them being there. Seeing the beer didn't help. She didn't want to take off her clothes to put pajamas on, so she crawled under the covers in her bed still wearing her royal blue leggings and a long shirt covered in a large unicorn and butterflies. Then she went back to working on the gift she was crafting.

Eight o'clock, the card game was getting louder. She stole a peek at the boys when she came out of the bathroom. Gunner smashed the Jack of clubs onto a pile of cards and his face lit up. "Gotcha! I win ...somethin'. What do I win fellas?"

Mike glared at Gunner. "We ain't playin' for money, buddy. And the chips are all gone." He scraped his hand inside an empty plastic bowl to exaggerate the point.

Gunner laughed. "Must be bigger stakes around here than potato chips." He stood up and swayed, staring down at Vincent. Vincent seemed to catch something in Gunner's eye and rose slowly, a smile creeping across his bloated face.

"Yup, I'm bored. How's about we had a little fun." Vincent picked up his beer and drained the bottle. He banged it down on the table and wiped a dribble from his chin with the back of his hand. "Could use a filly about now. I ain't got none since Debbie Smith blew me behind the dance hall two weeks ago. How about you, Gunner...wanna go find some fillies?"

Mike gave his friends a lop-sided grin and started to say goodbye. He appeared glad to see them go and would probably be happy to flop into bed and sleep off the beer.

Then he laid his head on the kitchen table. Within seconds he was out cold.

Eight twenty-seven, a piercing scream jerked him awake. "What the fuck? Doris! Are you okay?" He stumbled into her room.

"He made me do it!" Doris screamed. The covers of her bed had been torn away. Blood covered her sheets, her unicorn and butterflies splattered red. Vincent stood dumbstruck, gawking at

Gunner. He was lying on his back across her bed, his hands to his face screaming in pain.

That was the last day that Doris saw herself as a princess. A warrior, yes. No doubt about that. Forced to defend herself, the feelings of love and protection her family had provided were forever lost. She'd no more illusions of being a princess. The taunting and jeers from her classmates, along with the loathsome glares of Gunner's two brothers and three of his sisters, dispelled that fantasy.

No one who looked at the blinded teenager could feel anything but pity for Gunner. The doctors had done their best to save his right eye, but the quills had been driven in too far and the barbs did further damage when in his drunken state, he had tried to pull them out. The eye had to be removed.

No one seemed to care that *the accident* happened while he was attempting to molest a little girl. They weren't there. They didn't see the horror that she was going through. Doris didn't have a scratch on her after all. How bad could it have been? A couple of boys having fun.

At that thought, Doris snapped her suitcase shut and flung it from the bed. It was bad enough that she had been ostracized all through school. Until she couldn't take it anymore and begged her mother and father to let her move away. Far, far away where no one knew her past. Where she might have a chance at a decent future.

When she turned seventeen, her parents relented. There were distant relatives in Maine, on the Aroostook Reservation. She moved the day after high school graduation, an honor student ready to take on the world. It owed her after all. Doris never went back to Eskasoni.

She scowled at her baggage and called the night porter. Other than higher education, Ben, with his categorical disregard for her past, was the only thing to which she ever returned. And he was always glad to see her. As he would be now. Perhaps he had called to ask her to come home. She put the strange woman out of her mind. If she could put a wager on it, she'd say Ben would take her back with open arms. He always did.

Chapter Ten

"My nose is cold," groaned Emily in sleepy wonder. The clank of the cast iron door woke her early Friday morning. Emily guessed from the dim light that it couldn't be later than six.

Ben, dressed in heavy cotton pants, a grey thermal shirt and wool socks, crouched in front of the woodstove, stuffing it with crumpled paper and thin slats of pine. It had gotten very cold indeed.

"Have you warm in no time," he said. He struck a match and lit the wad of paper. "Stay tucked in for a while and I'll make us some coffee."

"Mmm...coffee." Emily threw off the covers and leapt out of bed. "I'll make the coffee," she blurted out.

"You sure? It's no trouble...I'll get the Coleman stove going. Won't take a minute." Ben had the Coleman open on the table. An aluminum percolator sat beside it along with a can of generic ground coffee.

"I'm positive," said Emily. "I slept like a log, or a bear. And I'm as hungry as one, so don't mess with me."

She grabbed a plastic jug from an open tote and thrust it at Ben. "You can get some fresh water for me though. Please," she added, softening her tone.

She could already feel the warmth emanating from the woodstove. Ben looked hungry too. He seemed to be feasting his eyes on her firm round breasts. She could feel her taut nipples straining against the soft fabric of the long johns. "The water...Ben?"

"Yes, right...right away," he stammered. Then he bolted out the door.

Emily went to the woodstove and put another log in the fire. "You girls are going to get me into trouble...at least I hope so," she whispered into her bosom.

The effect they had on Ben hadn't escaped her and she was delighted by his reaction. His face turned red as a beet when she caught him ogling her. It was nice to be the centre of attention for a change.

Her last romantic interval had been six months ago and lasted less than a week. Two dinners and a movie. Big deal. What went wrong? Then she remembered. No chemistry. He was cute enough, whatever his name was, but there were no sparks. She didn't even like his voice. It was too high pitched for her liking and he had a terrible habit of giggling when he was nervous, which turned her off completely. Calvin, that was it...or Colton, something like that. Talk about lasting impressions, she couldn't even remember his name. She didn't think Ben would be so easy to forget.

Emily carefully measured out the coffee while she reminisced. She found a salt shaker and added a dash to the grounds. Then Ben came inside with the jug of water and passed it to her. She passed back a shy smile and thanked him.

"You're not dressed." He moved quickly over to the bunks and started to straighten the beds.

"Very astute," said Emily. She bit her lip and looked down at her frumpy attire. She meant to ignore him, but couldn't pass up the opportunity. She wasn't sure why. Hillary told her that sarcasm, being the lowest form of wit, should be avoided at all costs.

May as well tell me not to breathe. It was something quite beyond her control, she really meant no harm and hoped others could see that.

She poured water into the percolator, dropped the metal basket inside and put on the lid. Then she lit a match, turned the knob on the Coleman stove and lit the burner. She adjusted the flame and put the pot on top of it. When she turned around Ben had his duffle bag on top of his bunk and was rooting through the contents as if he were looking for something important.

"Sorry, Ben. I don't function well in the morning before my coffee. I'll get dressed now while it's brewing. Did you find what you were looking for?"

"My toothbrush...I forgot to pack a toothbrush. How mindless of me!" He put his hands on his hips and shook his head.

Emily brought out the suitcase from under her bunk and opened it. She unzipped a small cosmetics bag, took out a toothbrush, still in its package, and handed it to Ben. "Here. Caitlyn didn't pack me a decent pair of pajamas, but she made sure I had a new toothbrush. I have a travel toothbrush in my purse that I can use. Do you have paste?"

"Paste?" said Ben.

"Toothpaste...do you have any?" Emily rolled her eyes and went to get her slouch purse. She'd hung it under her jacket on a hook jutting out of the wall by the door. She dug inside and pulled out a plastic case and a small tube of Colgate.

Ben found his voice again. "I don't want to put you out."

"You're not. Now, if you can give me a minute, I'll get dressed." She shooed him out the door and went back to her suitcase. She took out a pair of faded jeans and looked for a T-shirt. Caitlyn had packed three of the tightest ones she owned with low necklines. No sports bra. Nothing but under-wires and padding. Emily scowled. *Caitlyn! I know what you're thinking.*

Emily chose the black T-shirt, no bra. She would be wearing one of the thick wool sweaters Ben brought for her and besides, she was camping. She didn't mind going au naturel. She was sure her interview subject wouldn't mind either. Time to get down to business. She finished dressing, brushed her teeth and poured two cups of fairly palatable coffee. Today promised to be wild beyond her imagination. She wanted to be prepared, if that were possible.

"Great coffee," said Ben. "Job's yours. Mine usually tastes like tar, or worse."

"Oh, it's worse, trust me," said Emily. She flashed him an evil grin and stuffed another piece of cinnamon bun in her mouth. They were having a quick bite before heading out.

Tommy and Michelle left before dawn to find a blind to hide in. Ben told her that early morning hunts usually bore good results, but as they hadn't returned yet, it was assumed there'd been no show of moose.

"Tommy will come find me if he gets anything. He's the only one among us besides Michelle who is allowed to shoot one," said Ben. "But, he won't be able to handle it himself, even with Michelle there."

"But you have a gun. Is it just for protection then...you know, coyotes and bears?" Emily checked her battery supply and changed new ones into her camera to be on the ready. She was eager to get started.

"I have a license for bear. But in all the times I've been up here only one has crossed my path. And I didn't shoot it. Like I said. I don't like the taste of bear that much and I'm not going to kill anything I can't eat. There's a bounty on coyotes, but I won't eat them either so I usually avoid them if I can." Ben finished off his roll and slugged back the rest of his coffee.

"So why do you come up here? I thought the whole idea of being a hunter was being able to kill something. You don't get to do that." Emily was beginning to wonder why they were there at all.

"I can participate in any other way, which means everything else pertaining to the care and preparation of the carcass. A moose is a big animal," Ben explained. "It's a big job. But with an animal that size and seven or eight hundred pounds of meat on the line, well worth the effort. Feeds a lot of people." He gave her a wink and a nod that said hurry up then picked up a tan colored knapsack.

Emily quickly cleared the table while Ben grabbed a container of mixed nuts with dried fruit and some juice packs out of the cooler. He stuffed it all in the knapsack. It was time to go.

Chapter Eleven

Wesley, Me. Friday morning.

Doris didn't recognize the little blue Colt parked in Ben's driveway. She spied the SUV sitting beside Ava's Prius and came to the same conclusion. Covertly, she backed down the lane and pulled into the narrow path that led to Ben's hunting lodge. If anyone drove by, her car would be invisible behind a swath of hawthorn trees and alders.

When she reached Ava's house on foot she faced the kitchen at the rear of the house and smiled when she saw that the window over her sink had been left open. She boldly planted herself under the sill and stood slowly until she could see inside. Ava faced a middle-aged woman whose head seemed to be stuck in the refrigerator. She watched as the older woman shooed her out of the way and took a small vial of liquid out of the refrigerator door. Their agitated voices carried through the room and out the window.

"This one," Ava said. "I swear my eyes are better than yours, Rosie. Ben got that one a month ago. This is the fresh vial here."

"But there's still a dose of insulin in this one, Ava. It hasn't expired you know."

"I don't care," insisted Ava. "I want the fresh one. Throw that in the trash, now please."

Rosie obeyed then ordered Ava in turn to lean over the sink. Doris ducked down out of sight, but held her position under the sill.

"Why can't I have it in my stomach like I always do? Or my leg?"

"You know there's no muscle left in your abdomen," admonished the nurse. "And right now I feel like giving you a good jab in the arse for giving me your cold and for being so stubborn, so hike up your skirt and bend over."

Ava apparently couldn't argue with that so she complied, but as soon as her administrations were finished she dismissed Rosie with instructions to phone before calling in on her over the weekend. Ben may be home early from his trip and she might not need her help.

Doris stood again as the voices faded. Rosie gave Jack a pat on the head. He stayed with Ava when Ben went on extended trips. Then the nurse picked up her belongings, gave Ava a quick peck on the cheek and left through the front door.

Doris would have made her retreat then, but seeing Ava go to a closet and take out a raglan and a stout cane, she waited. What was the old woman up to? Her interest grew when Ava tottered over to the front window and peeked outside.

Her instincts were confirmed when she heard Ava call out to the dog.

"Come on, Jackie boy. The coast is clear. Let's see if you're any good at sniffing out weasels."

At the first sign of Ava taking her coat from the closet, Jack had been up and wagging his tail expectantly at the front door. She opened it now and the hound ran out. "Go get him, Jack!"

Doris slinked around to the side of the house and watched as Ava tottered down the gravel lane. Taking a path behind the homestead she came to the small refurbished red barn situated between the two Blackheart properties. Ben had added a chicken coop on the lee side of the barn. A low wire fence encompassed a large field surrounding the outside. Not that it presented any boundary for his hens. They free-ranged and fluttered over it with ease.

Doris took up position on the opposite side of the building knowing she must be ahead of Ava. She was surprised to see the old woman stride up the lane with a determined look on her face and turn in towards the barn. She heard the hinged door open and then Ava's footsteps trodding gingerly over the uneven floorboards.

A hatched door beside the woodpile inside gave access to the chickens' nest boxes. Perhaps she just came to get eggs after all. But then, why the cane? A small window on the opposite side of the barn provided a clear view of Ava. She opened the coop door and picked up an egg, then laid it down again. Ave hadn't brought a basket to put the eggs in and appeared to be casting her eyes over the barn, looking for something to put them in.

Jack was no doubt eager to see his master and had scampered on down the lane. He would come back when he found no one at home.

The barn held a chaos of woodcutting devices, ropes and chains, buckets and barrels. Dark stained coveralls hung from hooks in the wall. A pegboard contained coils of wire and a variety of hand tools that all bore signs of age and heavy usage. Tin cans, most of them filled with nails and screws or nuts and bolts, covered a roughly hewn shelf underneath the montage. Several cages and an assortment of traps took up space in a far corner. Doris couldn't make out the contents in the opposite space. Dirty rags were strewn everywhere.

Ava's gaze settled on a piece of blue flannel bunched up beside a pile of sawdust on the floor. She took her cane over to the rag and hitched it off the floor. Then she raised the sturdy rod and slid the remnant down its length until it reached her waiting hand. She leaned her cane against the shelf and shook dust out of the square of cloth.

Jack came sniffing in the door and Ava spoke to him, her voice cutting through the quiet morning air. "This will do. What a shame no one is around to see how clever I am. Sharp as ever. I wish Benny could see that and stop worrying about me so much. Forty years old and no wife, no grandchildren either," she muttered. "I wonder who this Emily girl is that Benny took hunting with him? Well, Jack, that's a first. He must be interested in her."

Ava appeared to sigh as Jack dashed off to do some more exploring. She took the piece of flannel back to the woodpile, laid it across a couple of logs and carefully placed six freshly laid eggs in the middle of the square. She brought up the corners and tied them in a loose knot. She was about to pick up the fragile package when a chicken came fluttering through the open barn door at a startling pace, squawking in distress.

"Jack!" shouted Ava. "Stop chasing these poor chickens!"

The Bantam hen veered sharply and skid into the woodpile, a flash of dark fur in close pursuit. It wasn't Jack. Two quick, black eyes stopped dead at Ava's boot clad feet, then dashed into the pile of loosely stacked logs. The hen, in its witless state, had missed seeing the open coop door and instead of fleeing safely inside, had clawed her way to the top of the logs.

"You bugger!" Ava screamed at the woodpile. "Come out of there, right now!" Apparently, she'd quite forgotten about the weasel, but having nearly collided with the verminous creature, recalled her greater purpose. A wave of fury washed over the gaunt figure making her tremble.

She turned and tottered over to the rugged shelf to retrieve her cane. The chicken, now statuesque, glared down at Ava. The weasel, hidden amongst the logs, cowered down to wait her out. The infuriated old woman was having none of it.

Ava raised her cane and brought it down on a piece of knotty pine, no doubt in hopes of startling the predator out of its hiding place.

Much to her chagrin, the tap produced by the strike of her cane wouldn't have startled a field mouse, much less a conniving full grown weasel. Doris could see that Ava simply didn't have the strength to accomplish the deed.

Infuriated, Ava dropped the cane and grabbed a piece of wood midway up through the pile. She shimmied it out and let it fall to the floor with a thud. Some of the logs shifted position and tumbled inward to take up the space. It was enough to make the hen think better of her perch and flutter down to the sawdust strewn floorboards. Still no sign of the weasel. The bird made her escape out the barn door.

"Come out of there you varmint? I know you're in there!" shouted Ava through quivering lips.

She pried up on another log higher up in the pile. It was almost eye level to Ava and she was having trouble getting it to budge. Then she put her hands around the end of the log and pulled.

It came out in a rush. Ava let go. Too late, the momentum knocked her sideways and she tumbled to the floor. No sound came from the pile of logs. Not one shift. In fact, other than the sound of Ava's pounding heart, the barn was deathly quiet under the late morning sun.

Chapter Twelve

When they got out of the half-ton, Ben reached behind his seat and took out two blaze orange vests. "Here you go," he said. "So *we* don't get shot!"

Emily stood on the bank of one of Ben's favorite lookout points. The view across the barrens, flanked by a balsam forest, spanned nearly a mile. The words barely parted his lips before two gun shots in quick succession split the air.

"Let's go see." Ben opened Emily's door and gave her a boost back into the truck.

Up until the lookout, the road had been well graded, but it deteriorated quickly from there. So deep were some of the tire tracks in places Emily feared they would slip into one of the ruts and get stuck. A few moments later Ben lumbered the truck onto a side road that flattened out and ended in a wide berth of gravel and hard packed dirt.

A black pickup sat parked in the middle of the cul-de-sac with the driver's side door left open. Two little legs hung out of the door and Emily could tell right away they belonged to a little girl. An older man and a younger man stood by the truck.

"Do you know them?" Emily asked.

"No, I don't think so." Ben pulled up on the far side of the truck away from where the men were standing. "I'm going to see what they got. Stay here for a minute."

Emily rolled down her window and twisted about in her seat so she could watch the proceedings. The older man was giving the younger one instructions on how to use his portable radio equipment when Ben rounded the corner. He nodded at the older man, smiled and stuck out his hand.

"I'm Ben. We heard shots. That you?"

The man grasped Ben's hand and shook it firmly. "I'm Patch, this here is my son Joey and my niece. Her mom's real sick. My wife is staying with her until we get back to Milford. There was no one to watch Justine so we brought her along. She's no trouble though, are you sweetheart," he drawled with affection. No reply came from the front of the pickup. "She's real shy," said Patch. "Come on I'll show you."

Patch took a large coil of grungy, grey rope from the back of the pickup and the three men walked off towards the edge of the scrub brush that banked down away from the road. Ben turned back and waved at Emily to let her know it was okay to come out. Then he followed the two men over the bank.

Emily jumped down from the half-ton and came around to the front of the pickup. A pair of pink sneakers and black leggings slid off the driver's seat and a small child appeared beside her. The girl's eyes were almond shaped and dark with lashes that swept up and touched her brow. Long black pigtails hung down her back. Emily guessed her to be no more than five or six. The child took a few tentative steps in the direction her uncle had gone in. Her fists were buried deep in the pockets of her hoodie and she looked as though she were about to cry.

Emily looked down at the forlorn little girl and smiled. "What's your name?"

"Justine," the girl answered. Then she cast her liquid black eyes to the ground. "What ...what's yours?" she ventured when Emily made no effort to turn away.

"Just Emily," said Emily.

Justine looked up and giggled.

"Want to go see?" Emily reached for her hand. Justine grabbed hold and they walked over together to see what the men were up to. Emily saw little but tree stumps and scrub brush when she reached the edge of the bank.

The men were almost two hundred feet away. Joey stayed behind with the moose carcass and one of the walkie talkies while the two older men picked their way back through the clear cut laying out a long line of rope behind them.

"Want to wait back in the truck where it's warmer?" Emily saw that the little girl was shivering. She also wanted to get her camera and have it ready for when the moose appeared.

"Sure," said Justine. "I'm cold."

Patch waved at them when came he came back to his pickup to tie the end of the rope to a hitch under his tailgate. He jumped in and slowly turned down the open road dragging the rope behind until it was taut. Then he began to tow the moose out of the clear cut.

Ben waited patiently, observing from a knoll jutting up from the bank. A rope under extreme tension was a lethal force. He hoped it wouldn't break and he was thankful that Emily and the little girl were inside his truck out of harm's way. There'd been one delay when the carcass got caught up on a tree stump. Other than that, Patch managed to drag the beast over the final fifty yards without incident.

Ben clambered down the knoll eager to help the men wrest the moose into position at its base. By propping the animal's upper body on the incline, the blood and gut pile could flow out largely unaided by anything more than gravity.

Patch took the lead, spreading the front legs. Ben and Joey struggled to keep the carcass from sliding. Patch looked up exasperated and held up his weary knife. The tough moose hide wouldn't yield to the blade. "Dull as shit, wouldn't you know," he spat.

Ben swiftly extracted a knife, razor sharp, from its sheath at his hip and passed it to the older man. He then walked to the back of his half-ton and plucked out a rather long rawhide sack. He stopped to wave at the girls inside, then strolled casually back to the hunters.

Emily took in Ben's slow, languid gait. He seemed to emanate a gentle yet commanding air to all in his presence. From the sack he took out a long hunting knife, a small hand saw and three large steel hooks equipped with T-shaped handles. Then he rolled up his sleeves.

Emily watched the garish scene peripherally as she chatted with Justine. She had never seen any great amount of blood or the butchering of an animal, though she harbored a faint memory of her father skinning a rabbit and making a stew. Mostly she remembered the cooking smells. The memory made her nose wrinkle. She was relating the experience to Justine when they heard a loud gush, followed immediately by a boisterous cheer.

"They got the guts out!" bellowed Justine.

"Indeed." Emily regarded the muddy red rivulets that pooled and drained around a bulbous form that jiggled like jelly on the ground a few feet away from the dead animal.

Ben stayed busy cutting into the rear end of the moose by its tale. When finished, he lifted out a circle of fur-embedded muscle and passed it to Joey.

"First kill, you have to wear the bracelet. Isn't that right, Patch?"

Patch gave Ben a knowing wink and agreed the tradition, as a rite of passage, should be observed. "That's right, Joey. First kill. You won the right to wear it."

Joey took the circle of fur gingerly with his thumb and index finger and laid it behind him upside the knoll. He then thrust two fingers into the still warm moose carcass and trailed a thick smear of blood down one side of his cheek.

Ben looked up at Joey and grinned. "I never wore the bracelet either."

Joey grinned back.

Emily hadn't been able to keep the little girl away from the carnage any longer. They closed in on the group in time to witness the exchange. A broad smile dimpled Justine's face as she looked up at her cousin.

Patch swelled with pride. "Joey, you may only be eighteen, but you're nowhere between a boy and a man. Now that you made your first moose kill, no one will ever doubt that you are a man. You did well, son."

With the aid of Ben's malevolent looking meat hooks, the men then hauled the beast into the pickup and secured the tailgate. Then Emily cajoled Joey into posing for pictures. She took stock of her work – Joey, his blood smeared face jutting forward, even white teeth bared brazenly toward the camera, gripping the massive, lifeless head with its meaty tongue protruding and grotesque. One day in the Highlands and she had already been witness to a moose kill. Emily could hardly believe her luck.

She wondered about the discarded gut pile as they turned around and headed back to camp to meet Tommy and Michelle. A macabre feast for some of the local carnivores came to mind and she squirmed at the thought.

Ben noticed her slight shudder. "You cold?"

He'd taken her appreciative smile as a yes.

"Actually, I'm fine. I was wondering about the gut piles and the wildlife they must…"

Ben looked back to the road when Emily didn't finish her sentence. Not fifty feet ahead, in the left-hand ditch, lay her answer. A moose had been shot only a few miles from where they found Patch, Joey and Justine. Six bald eagles made short work of ripping the bag of organs apart and clawing out long green trails of viscera.

"Eagles! Can we stop?" Emily was already digging for her camera.

Ben pulled over on the right side of the road just twenty feet from the kill site. He took the opportunity to unbuckle her seatbelt and reach across her to unlatch her door. She smelled like cinnamon and he longed to slip his tongue between her lips, to taste her mouth.

Easy, down boy. Not the time or place to be thinking about doing Miss Spitfire. He quietly nudged her door open. She inched her way out and approached the lurid scene snapping pictures as she walked. Ben thought she looked adorable in her faded jeans and green rubber boots, wisps of long auburn hair blowing across her face. She looked dismayed when all the eagles suddenly soared to the tree tops.

"I think I've had enough," she yelled to him while strutting back to the truck.

Ben heaved a great sigh when she settled in beside him, brushing his arm with hers as she stuffed the camera back in her purse. *I could never get enough of you, Emily.*

The sun sprawled over the camp when they returned near noon. Tommy's truck sat parked next to the tent trailer but there was no sign of him or Michelle.

"They're probably sleeping," said Ben as he backed in beside the Ritz. "Are you tired?"

"No, and I'm not hungry. Justine and I helped ourselves to juice and the snacks you brought. She's such a dear. I'm glad you asked them to visit us if they come back over the weekend."

Emily gathered the empty containers, her purse and the tan knapsack while Ben came around to open her door and help her out. "I can make you a grilled cheese or something if you like though. You must be starved."

Ben opened the trailer door for her and they went inside. "I could eat, but I don't want you going to any trouble. I can fend for myself. I'm quite capable."

Emily's tone became playful. "Well, it's a wonder you're alive then. If you fend for yourself as well as you make coffee, that is."

"Brat!" Ben grabbed her sweater and pulled her towards him. Reaching underneath he dug his fingers under her ribcage causing Emily to shriek and twist in his arms. She was laughing uncontrollably by the time she fell to the floor flushed and damp from exertion, panting for breath.

"That will teach you," Ben huffed.

He wasn't completely undone by the scuffle but she'd given him strong resistance, causing his heart to race. Her strength surprised him. He was a little sore from helping Patch and Joey, but, of course, he'd gotten the better of her.

Emily leaned back and gazed up at Ben staring down at her, smoothing his disheveled hair in place with one hand.

"You're a bloody mess, mate," said Emily when she could finally speak again. "I hope you didn't get any on me."

Indeed, Ben's pants were streaked with ruddy brown stains and his thermal shirt sleeves were tinged with a rosy hue up to the elbows. Slivers of dried blood stuck in the skin under and around his fingernails. He looked down at his attire and shirked his shoulders.

"Tommy and I usually wash up in the creek. I guess I should go now." He offered his hand to help her up but Emily scrambled out of reach.

"Not so fast." She stood up by her bunk and hauled the heavy knit sweater over her head. The deep blue fibers were still clean, but when she inspected her thin black T-shirt and her skin underneath, the blood from Ben's fingers was evident.

"Did you want to come?" he asked softly.

Emily's pulse quickened. Maybe she didn't hear him right. Or in the right context. In the heat of the moment...of course she took him the wrong way. What was she thinking?

"Oh no. I'm not bathing in freezing cold water! I don't think I'm that hardy. Maybe I could use the large tote you brought the bedding in. I could heat some water and fill that up for a quick tub bath."

"Absolutely. What a great idea," said Ben. "I'll bring in the rest of the water that we picked up last night and you can bail it into some pans on the Coleman."

Emily thanked him and went to rummage through the kitchen cupboards. She found two aluminum pots that would both fit on the burners, poured the morning's leftover water into them and lit the portable stove. She opened the door for Ben and he carried in the tote still heavy with several gallons of spring water. To her surprise the water was tepid, heated by the morning sun.

"This won't take long," said Emily. "The water is already warm. Why don't you use it after me? I'm not that dirty – a little sweaty maybe. And…" she faltered.

"And what?" Ben topped up the pans with water, filling them almost to the brim.

"And, I don't want you to go and leave me here alone," said Emily. We're not even sure if your friends are here. They may be out for a walk or gone with someone else. It's not like we checked to see where they were."

"Come with me," he commanded gently.

Emily followed him out the door and they walked towards Tommy's tent trailer. They got as far as the woodpile, centered between the two camps, when she heard them. Loud snores emanating from the open windows. Emily's hand flew up to her mouth. She stifled a laugh before turning and sprinting back towards their more stationary quarters.

"I know Tommy," said Ben when he caught up with her. "He'll get up around one or two and then goof around for the afternoon before going out again, closer to dusk. Michelle will do whatever he does."

"I'm sorry, but I'm still nervous." Emily checked the water and decided it was hot enough for bathing.

She didn't want Ben to leave and told him so. Both his friends were sound asleep and if her screams of protest and laughter hadn't jostled them just moments ago, then they were unlikely to wake until they were good and ready to do so, despite any crisis that may occur. Not that being left naked in a tub of hot water constituted a crisis, but anything could happen.

"Bandits, bears, coyotes – take your pick. Then you'd have a far worse fate. Facing my sister to tell her you weren't there to save me. You poor thing. I shudder to think what she would do to you."

"Well, since you put it that way, I guess I can stick around and clean up after you. We'll need a lot more water later. We can go together then."

Emily flashed him an appreciative smile. He took a container of soap and a towel from his duffle bag and passed it to her. Then he left through the open door. She shut it tight, feeling a sudden chill without the sun's heat flooding in. She placed the rubber tub in the space between the bunks and poured in the warmed water. Then she stripped and slid deep inside the narrow enclosure.

After bathing, she patted herself dry gingerly not knowing if Ben had thought to pack more than one towel. A tap came from the door just as she finished dressing.

"Come in. I was just finishing up." Emily swept her hair into a ponytail then looked up to see Ben leaning in through the doorway.

She had put on a pair of black jeans and a red knit T-shirt that clung to her cool, damp skin. She was about to pull the blue sweater over her head, but thought to check the temperature outside first. It was already getting hotter inside with the addition of Ben's heated stare.

Ben stepped inside and sat on one of the padded benches. "The kids are up." He tried to avoid looking directly at her, but he was drawn by her lean, curvaceous physique. "Why don't you join them while I clean up and then we'll all have a bite – unless you want to stay and help me clean up?"

He caught the damp towel Emily tossed at him while she headed for the door. "And have the neighbors talking about me behind your naked back. I don't think so. See you outside," she tittered and left closing the door behind her.

Ben was left toying with the damp towel and chiding himself for being so brash. She was even more beautiful, if it were possible, with her hair swept up. Shorter wisps fell in curls around her brow and cheeks, giving her a childlike air.

But, the way she looked at him. Innocent and beguiling, as though unaware of her radiant sexuality. Ten years ago, he'd have bedded her by now. What virtue was there in denying himself a little fun now? And Emily? She'd said it herself, she didn't have a boyfriend. This was a battle of his own design – falling all over her one minute, then fighting to keep her chaste in the very next – one he couldn't possibly win. She slew him at every turn.

Emily stepped outside. Michelle waved her over towards the camp chairs where she sat shucking the husks from long ears of corn. The native woman was stout and amply endowed, dressed in track pants and a plain orange sweatshirt.

"Come here Em, darling," she hollered. "Ben says you got lucky this morning. Come tell me all about it. Trying to get information out of him is like trying to shoe a chicken isn't it? I don't know how you're going to get a story out of the likes of him."

Emily plopped down beside her and sighed. "It was pretty amazing for me though I can see how nonplussed Ben would be, having done this so many times before. I guess it was just work to him. Work he likes to do, obviously. No one had to ask him, he just jumped right in."

"That's Ben...salt of the earth. Wait till you get to know him better. He'd do you proud girl. You're not hitched to another are you? S'pose I should ask before I start matchmaking, though by the way you look at him, I'd bet my right arm you're single."

"Well, your arm is safe but I'm not really looking for a relationship right now. I'm quite focused on my work for the moment. Maybe in the future…"

The slam of a screen door preceded Tommy skulking away from his trailer. His exaggerated walk reminded Emily of a Sumo wrestler. He held at arm's length a large roll of toilet paper with several sheets streaming like a white ribbon behind him in the breeze.

"He may look like he's sneaking off, but he slammed that door to make sure we saw him," laughed Michelle. "There's another good salt. He'll do anything for a laugh."

"I know," said Emily. "Ben did warn me about him."

Both women were still laughing when Ben sauntered out of the Ritz wearing faded Levis and another grey thermal shirt, this one clean with missing buttons. He'd rolled up his sleeves exposing bulging muscles and freshly scrubbed flesh.

"We'd better get some lunch ready," said Michelle. "The boys should be ravenous by now. Give me a hand getting up darling. Like 'em or not we got to take care of them, eh?"

"Amen," said Emily. "They're a lot of work most of them."

"Yes, but if you find one that makes you laugh every day and you decide to make him your vocation, like I have with Tommy, you'll have a happy life. You deserve as much don't you?"

"At the very least," said Emily, smiling wistfully.

She rose and took Michelle's hand. Nestled in the low slung chair, her ample bust fairly pinned her in the seat. With her bottom almost touching the ground, she was quite unable to get up by herself.

"Thanks darling. Ben said you were really nice. It breaks my heart to know he's so alone and sad all the time."

"What makes you think he's not happy? He has everything going for him as far as I can tell." Emily glanced over at Ben picking through the woodpile. The logs were too big to fit in the woodstove and it appeared that he meant to rectify the situation.

"I can tell by the way he looks at you that he's beginning to realize he's missing something. And I'm pretty sure it isn't Doris. She didn't do much for him, and maybe he didn't do much for her either. I don't know. But, Tommy said he was better off without her so I'm glad she's gone. He deserves to be happy too.

"He lost his dad in the spring. That was a bigger blow for him. He loved that old man with all his heart, that's for sure. Thank God Ava is holding on. Couples that have been together that long sometimes don't have the will to go on once they lose their partner. Ava's strong though. Stubborn as a mule too she is. God love her."

"I know about his dad. I lost both my parents in a car accident just before I graduated from high school." Emily teared at the memory, surprised by the flood of emotion that swept over her. It had been so long ago.

"There, there, darling," Michelle consoled her. "It's not something a child gets over, at any age."

Emily nodded her head and asked the question that now plagued her. "Doris...is she his ex-wife?"

"Girlfriend. Never married her. She left last winter after sponging off him for almost ten years. Never mind, girl. She's ancient history now."

"Good to know." For some reason unfathomable to her, Emily *was* glad to hear that. Too bad she felt so many leagues under him. She didn't think she could hold Ben's attention for anything close to permanency. She may be a pleasant diversion for him, but that would be the extent of it.

He would need a much more sophisticated woman, one with means that matched his own, to truly captivate him. She would have to be down to earth as well, and lord knows, environmentally conscious. Where on earth he would find such a person, she'd no idea. She didn't tell Michelle what she was thinking though. Why dispel the fantasy when she obviously enjoyed building suspense around the possibilities?

"Don't count him out Em, darling." She nudged Emily in the shoulder for emphasis. "Ben has been hunting for love a long time. He just won't admit it. Same as you. Anything could happen."

The women joined forces then and whipped up a satisfying meal. Michelle's homemade baked beans went well with the boiled corn and some store bought fish cakes. Tommy helped himself to the last piece of sourdough bread and sopped up the rest of his bean sauce with it. They were eating outside and when he tossed his empty plate into the fire pit, everyone followed suit.

Emily hadn't been for a run in quite a few days and was itching to stretch her legs. Ben agreed to take her for a long walk, insisting that it wouldn't be safe for her to run off by herself.

She had to concede, having inappropriate footwear to begin with. A walk in the wilderness with Ben would be a marvelous concession.

Tommy and Michelle decided to do some more scouting and look for a better location for a blind they could use that evening. Ben took his binoculars from the half-ton and put the case in the tan knapsack along with two bottles of spring water. He checked his jacket pocket for shells and slung his rifle over his shoulder. Emily left her slouch purse under her mattress but took her camera. They both put on felt-lined rubber boots. Ben said there was snow in the deep woods and it would be much colder, so layers of clothing would be appropriate.

He didn't lie. As soon as they left the open road and started to trek into the forest, Emily noticed a dramatic change in temperature. They were walking in snow, not fresh powder and not the crystalized sort that crunched underfoot. Instead it was like walking on a bed of soft moss that absorbed their footprints without much change in composition. It wasn't long before Emily started to notice piles of brown pellets in the snow.

"Moose poop right!" She grinned at Ben when he nodded at them to make sure she noticed.

He was quiet again, which unsettled Emily. She wanted to talk to him, but felt out of place taking the lead, interrupting his solitude. Finally he stopped and pointed to a mushy black pile in the snow. "What animal do you suppose left that?"

"It must be a black bear," said Emily. "It doesn't look at all like moose buttons."

"Actually it probably was a bull moose. It's the time of year and the change in diet and behavior. The rut is almost over, but in full swing...makes a bull change in more ways than one. When he gets a whiff of cow in heat, he goes into a trance. His eyes glaze over and his neck muscles bulge twice their normal size." Ben walked backwards as he spoke hulking his arms over his head like antlers, protruding his neck and shoulder muscles. He gave her a vacant stare, a lecherous grin and then stopped. Suddenly he lunged forward.

Emily shrieked! Then she laughed and held her ground. He stopped inches from her face. "Picking up her scent, he could walk right past you and not know you exist."

"And if you stood in his way?" She sounded coy and hadn't meant to. Emily stepped to the side to put some distance between them. This close to his eyes, with his breath on her lips, it made her woozy. She barely heard his response as she grabbed the branch of a nearby tree to steady herself.

"Get in his way and you'd be lucky to live and tell the tale." Ben took her hand and turned into the path leading her behind him.

"I don't doubt it. The bull that Joey brought down was pretty massive. I wouldn't want to come across one – at any time of year."

She zeroed in on Ben's swagger as they continued walking single file, through a narrow trail undistinguishable to Emily. She longed to touch the flesh concealed inside the fabric of his worn weary jeans. A scene played in her mind to facilitate the fantasy when she tripped. She didn't see the snow covered root that the toe of her boot snagged. She lunged forward and twisted to take the fall on her side.

Ben whirled around. "You alright?"

She felt her face go crimson. He helped her up. Then he saw the offending root.

"Walk on the outsides of your feet. You won't trip so easily."

Emily tried the new approach and found she was better able to keep her balance on the uneven terrain. She also liked the way her muscles responded to her exertions. Between the walking and the climbing, over and under fallen tree trunks and wayward limbs, she was getting a full workout. They stopped at one point when she protested at being overheated. Ben took the opportunity to take out the water bottles and stuff her jacket inside the knapsack.

"That's interesting." Emily chugged some of the cool liquid. "From the moose's perspective. I wonder what it's like for the female. Does she feel any different, especially the first time?"

"You'd have to ask her. How would I know how a bleeding cow moose felt?" A puzzled grin accompanied the remark. He didn't wait for a reply, simply turned on his heel and led her out of the thicket to a meadow at the peak of the plateau. Beyond lay a broad valley. Ben dug his binoculars out of the knapsack. He scanned the valley below and paused when he came to a logging road some distance away. Nearby stood a group of small copses that gave nothing away to the naked eye.

Emily stared in the direction Ben pointed to as he passed her the binoculars.

"The small group of trees nearest the road. Do you see it?"

"I think so...something black with long legs. Nothing I can get a picture of."

"I guess not. Too bad though. This bugger must be fifteen hundred pounds. He's got a massive rack but he's hiding most of it behind those trees."

"I still don't see much."

"Here, let me see. Are you focused...in?" He paused. "Emily?"

"Yes?"

"Do I have two sooty circles around my eyeballs?"

"Yes. As a matter of fact, you do. Do I?"

"Yes."

"Tommy!" They shouted in unison.

"Wait till I get my hands on that scoundrel. Sometimes I swear, I could throw him in a gut pile." Ben was irked, but smiling, being quite familiar with his friend's harmless pranks.

"You take the arms and I'll take the legs. We'll toss him together!"

Emily couldn't help but laugh. They looked ridiculous as it was, but then Ben rubbed his eyes, enhancing his raccoon-like appearance. He was laughing now too and trying to wipe the soot off his hands with Emily's pant legs. She held him at bay, backing onto the edge of the plateau, dodging his advances, shrieking to the top of her lungs.

Ben backed off when Emily came close to the edge of the cliff and was surprised when she advanced on him like a mischievous bandit out for revenge. A worthy adversary. He so admired her tenacity even if she could still use a little taming. He feigned a fall, thrusting his foot out and hooking it behind her ankle. She toppled over him in a heap.

Before she could pull away, Ben quickly flipped her on her back and clapped his hand over her mouth, one leg slashed across hers from thigh to foot, pinning her in the snow covered ground. "Sssh, you'll scare all the game away for the next ten miles."

He looked down and was lost. Lost in those deep brown eyes, searching for her acquiescence, not caring anymore whether he had it or not, he raised his hand...and kissed her.

At first Emily felt stunned by the touch of his lips on her own. Not that she meant to stop him. He was kissing her – a deep, passionate kiss, devouring her lips, his tongue suckling and licking, darting then slow inside her mouth. Heat welled inside her as blood rushed to places in her body that, for the most part, had been dormant for far too long in Emily's mind. She closed her eyes and surrendered to the feeling. Then she kissed him back.

Chapter Thirteen

Only an hour left before dark, Tommy and Michelle left promptly to sit in the blind they discovered earlier. The snow was peppered with fresh sign all around. Tommy did a Tarzan beat on his chest and hollered from the back of his truck before they left. He vowed to bring at least one of the beasts home.

Emily huddled in her camp chair beside Ben's around the fire pit watching layers of grey and lavender cloud drift across the sky.

"Look there," said Ben. "What do you see?"

The upper layers were a blur, a fast moving mass of dark grey cloud. Beneath them, everything moved in slow motion. Pointing a finger at the sky, Emily described a scene unfolding.

Her vision began with a single cloud, an alligator elbow deep in a shallow swamp. The jaws thinned and stretched forward to form a trunk. The head grew bigger and sprouted ears that reminded her of a flying elephant. Slowly the trunk grew, longer and thinner, spiraling upwards while the ears shrank back. "Now, it's a unicorn charging through the sky. Look! It reached the dark bank of clouds blowing in from the east...and the mythical creature enters the stampede and disappears."

"That's quite the imagination, girl. I was going to say it looked like snow coming," said Ben.

That earned him a playful punch in the arm. They both laughed going inside the camp to look for something to eat.

"Do you really think it's going to snow? The forecast said clear weather last I heard. This will blow over, right?" said Emily. The thought unnerved her and she wanted to be reassured that they would return home on schedule. Sunday night she intended to be in her own bed.

"Yes, but that was two days ago. The Highlands' weather can change in a heartbeat. I've been in a blizzard up here in September. Stuck for three days. You just never know."

"I can't be stuck here!" Panic seethed inside her. "You can't do this to me!"

Emily didn't appreciate Ben's lax attitude over an impending storm. Hadn't told him about the appointment with a tradesman Monday morning. Not that it was any of his business. She had work to do, an assignment to finish, deadlines to meet.

Did the magazine even know she'd been taken out of the country? She doubted it. As a contributing writer she didn't live a nine to five existence at the office. No one would think anything amiss if they didn't hear from her for a day or two, or three! As long as she produced the caliber of work expected of her she had pretty much free reign to come and go as she pleased. But, of course, there were deadlines.

Ben put down the knife he was sharpening on a piece of flat, charcoal-colored stone. But instead of slicing the block of cheese he'd taken from the cooler, he put it down and stepped outside. Her harsh tone did well to kill his appetite.

He went to the woodpile and picked up his axe. Emily's outburst procured no response, because he couldn't think of a thing to say that would help the situation. In truth, there was nothing he could do about the weather and he didn't know if it would snow or not. It would snow if it wanted to. Nothing he could say would change that so he decided it better to say nothing at all. He certainly wasn't going to stand there and argue with her over the weather.

They needed logs split for the fire. Ben wouldn't let Emily get cold. He would feed her and keep her warm. She would interview him and he would entertain her. How surprised he was when she kissed him back on top of the plateau. Emily was full of surprises. Mostly pleasant so far Ben reckoned. He grinned and picked up another log to strike.

Alone with her thoughts, Emily took stock of her sparse accommodations. She lit the woodstove, thankful that Ben had prepared the kindling for them earlier in the day. She wasn't hungry anymore. Anxiety stymied her appetite. She wondered if Ben were feeling the same. She turned up the kerosene lantern and took out her notebook. She scanned the blank pages and sighed out loud. *He can't shut me out now. There's so much I need to ask him.*

Ben tapped on the door and came in with an armload of wood. Seeing her propped up on her pillow in the soft glow of the kerosene lantern made his heart leap. She was lying on her side, appearing long and curvaceous, writing in her notebook. She looked up, a timid smile forming on her lips.

"I'm sorry. I didn't mean to snap at you." She sounded truly contrite.

Ben went to the woodstove, dropped his load and put in a piece of seasoned maple. Then he picked up his duffle bag, rifled through it and brought out a harmonica. He sat on the edge of his bunk and blew softly into the wood and chrome plated instrument.

He peeked up at Emily. She had pulled herself up in the bunk and sat cross-legged with her notebook in her lap, her back to the wall.

A long tinny whine came from the harmonica, the high pitched note ending sharply and was followed by a deeper tone. A blues riff soon filled their cramped quarters and he took note of her humming along to the tune. Ben closed his eyes as he blew and sucked rhythmically on the instrument. Hearing her sing a few words, he peered over towards her and allowed the corners of his mouth to rise.

He played in earnest then, much louder and a little faster too. Emily abandoned her inhibitions and began to sing the Janis Joplin cover in a raspy voice resembling the ill-fated singer.

Oh Lord, won't you buy me a Mercedes Benz?
My friends all drive Porsches, I must make amends.
Worked hard all my lifetime, no help from my friends,

So Lord, won't you buy me a Mercedes Benz?

Oh Lord, won't you buy me a night on the town?
I'm counting on you, Lord, please don't let me down.
Prove that you love me and buy the next round,
Oh Lord, won't you buy me a night on the town?

Everybody!
Oh Lord, won't you buy me a Mercedes Benz?
My friends all drive Porsches, I must make amends,
Worked hard all my lifetime, no help from my friends,
So oh Lord, won't you buy me a Mercedes Benz?

Ben exaggerated the last note until it faded out with his breath. Then he passed the harmonica to Emily.

She shook her head. "I can't play."

"Well, you can certainly sing. I can teach you to play." He blew a few more notes into the instrument.

"Perhaps. I'm not completely tone deaf, but I've never tried to play anything before. Hillary is the natural. Plays piano, guitar and the clarinet, if you can believe that."

"I don't doubt you. She seemed quite competent in any of the dealings I've had with her." Ben looked straight into her eyes and added. "But she doesn't have your voice, or your beauty, does she?"

It wasn't really a question. A statement that begged debate perhaps, but he could tell Emily didn't care to slight his views just then. A shy smile revealed that she was enjoying his attention.

"I guess I should let you teach me."

"I intend to do just that," he assured her. Then he abolished the space between them and took her in his arms.

Within seconds, a loud bang on the thin metal door, followed by Tommy's unmistakable holler, interrupted what was meant to be an intimate embrace.

"Ben, come on! We got one!" He rapped twice more and yanked open the door.

Ben and Emily jumped up together though Emily looked unsure about what to do next. Ben simply reached for his coat and followed Tommy out the door. When he turned to close it he looked up at Emily and grinned.

"I'll be back...soon."

He stood transfixed as she stretched to ease the cramp in her legs then shook her hair out of the elastic that held her ponytail. "I'll heat some water," she said with a wink.

Her seductive smile made his knees weak. She blew him a kiss. He pretended to catch it and put it in his pocket. That's when Tommy yanked his arm and shoved him towards his truck.

"Come on man. I got a cow fifteen minutes' drive from here. We don't want her to get pinched by some luckless oafs driving by." They jumped in and Tommy tore down the lane panting with excitement.

"Michelle wouldn't stay there by herself. In case we got lost and couldn't find our way back to her. Silly woman. I know these mountains better than I know my own name."

"It's only her second time up isn't it?" Ben came to Michelle's defense sensing Emily would feel exactly the same way.

"I'm kidding you know. I wouldn't leave her up there by herself on any account. Don't know what I'd do if I lost her." Tommy fairly choked out the words.

Ben had never met two people who got along as well as Tommy and Michelle. The Grafton's came in a close second.

"How long you and Michelle been together now?" Ben knew it was over twenty years in all, but he wanted to hear Tommy's answer just the same. He knew what was coming.

"Been together forever of course. In our last lives we were wolves, me the alpha and Michelle was my bitch. And the one before that we were snowy owls…"

Tommy went on recounting all the lives he imagined they'd spent together, until they reached a particular thicket by the side of the road and he shut the truck down.

"Once you find your soul mate that's it then isn't it?" he concluded.

Ben got out of the truck scowling. "You think I'll ever find my soul mate, Tommy?"

"Michelle says you already have." Tommy winked at Ben and grabbed a skein of rope from the back of the truck. "Follow me."

Ben reached in Tommy's glove box, grabbed a flashlight and slammed the door. "Damn it, Tommy! That's a killer bog out there and it's freaking dark now. How am I supposed to find a soul mate and live happily ever after when you keep trying your best to get rid of me?"

"Tarnation Yankee! Why do you think I keep getting you to come up here with me? No one knows the bogs like you do. I'm frightened to death to go in there by myself. You do know that. Besides, this is where the damn cow got herself stuck and I had to put her out of her misery before she realized her predicament. I can't imagine the stress, hopelessly stuck in this never ending goop."

"Fine, fine. How far in? I'll lead."

"Just a couple of yards."

"Good."

"Good. That way. That's right. Right behind you, buddy." Tommy's voice quivered. He really was afraid of the bog.

"Come on. I see her now. It's not that bad. Pass me the rope."

"Whatever you say, Yank."

Emily put two pots of water on the woodstove. Then she took Michelle up on her invitation and joined her in the travel trailer. Michelle had already poured herself a glass of red wine and poured another for Emily as soon as she entered.

The glasses were stemmed, real glass. Nodding at them Michelle said, "can't leave all the luxuries of home behind can we now, darling?"

"Actually, you can. I just found that out." Emily related the events from the previous day, and those leading up to then, which culminated in her trip to the Highlands.

"See...I knew it. Ben is hot to trot for you honey. And Tommy – begging me to come up here with him. I knew something was up. Ah well, I'm glad I came. Nice to meet you Em, my darling."

The two women clinked glasses. Emily was glad she came too. It hadn't snowed, though it had gotten very cold. That fact alone took a great deal of stress off Emily's shoulders. No one would have to worry about the meat going bad either. Which meant the men would be in good spirits when they returned.

They went outside to light the campfire and wait. Few stars managed to twinkle through the thick patches of cloud that streamed across the sky. Together they gathered wood scraps near the chopping block Ben used earlier. Emily lit a match and held it under one of the paper plates that they covered in kindling.

It didn't take long for the fire to come to life, illuminating the camp for several feet in all directions. Emily could still see her breath it was so cold. She hunkered close to the warming flames after helping Michelle get settled in her seat, wrapped tight in a heavy wool poncho.

A long eerie howl pierced the air. Emily shot a glance over at Michelle.

"Coyotes. Place is polluted with them."

Emily went to the woodpile and brought an armful of split logs over to where they were sitting. She added a few to the fire and pulled her chair even closer to the flames.

"I wouldn't worry about them. They're more afraid of us than us of them."

"You think?"

"Well, most of us," Michelle laughed. "I can see this is all new to you. Don't forget, I have a gun and I know how to use it."

Emily had never heard coyotes in the wild before. After a few more howls she realized that the sounds must be covering a great distance and she relaxed a little. Still, she wished the men would hurry back. They seemed to be gone a dreadfully long time.

Emily thought to check the water heating on the woodstove. She didn't need the flashlight Michelle gave her to see her way across the clearing, but she used it regardless, feeling somewhat safer with a weighted object in hand.

Inside, the air was warm and the water hot enough to make tea, just above a gentle simmer. The fire had eaten up most of the wood she'd put in the woodstove. She moved the pots of water as far to the edge as possible and added a couple of small sticks, just enough so that the coals wouldn't completely die off.

She took her mobile phone out of her purse, thinking to check the time. There were no cellular towers to service the remote area they were in. She couldn't call or text anyone, but as her phone also served to tell date and time, she used it on occasion just for that purpose. Gaping at the blank screen now she realized that her battery was dead and she had no way to remedy that because she'd left her charger back at home in Bangor. Not that it mattered. It wasn't like she could plug her phone into a tree and recharge it.

She wondered if anyone had tried to reach her. Wondered even more what was taking Ben and Tommy so long. She tried to determine how long they'd been gone. It was well past the half hour of driving time she knew it would take. At least an hour more. How long could it possibly take to stuff a dead moose into the back of a truck?

She had an idea, having been witness to such an event just that morning. Then she remembered that the carcass needed to be bled and gutted before loading and that could take another hour with just the two men working on it. She flicked on the flashlight and went outside.

Michelle seemed relieved upon seeing her return. She picked obsessively at the fringe on her poncho, pulling out loose fibers and tossing them in the coals near her feet.

"I'm roasting here," she said when Emily approached.

Mindful of conserving the batteries inside, Emily turned the flashlight off once she passed the dark shadows of the woodpile. She helped Michelle up then and they repositioned their chairs further back from the now raging bonfire. Michelle had managed to toss in the rest of the logs Emily had brought over and stacked between them.

"When do you think they'll be back?" She could tell Michelle was also worried and wished there were something they could do to make the passage of time go quicker.

"Oh, they'll be back when they get here. I'd be troubled if Tommy was with anyone else. But with Ben, I don't worry so much. That man knows more about survival and the wilderness than half the men in Eskasoni. And that's saying a lot...for a white man," she added.

Then she said something that made Emily stiffen.

"It may take a little longer for them than I first figured. We had our sights on a young cow who crossed our path, but Tommy's gun jammed when he went to shoot her. She caught wind of us then and bolted into the bush.

"Well, we thought it was bush, but once we got out of the thicket we seen that she had run right into one of the killer bogs. There was nothing left to do. She couldn't get much further without getting hopelessly stuck, and by this time Tommy had replaced the jammed bullet, so he shot her."

Emily eyed Michelle's poncho sprawled across her lap, its fringe twisted in damp knots. "So, you're not afraid then?"

"Course not, darling. Ben will bring Tommy back to me. You'll see. He hasn't failed me yet." She sounded convincing, but her hands never stilled, twisting the fringe around and around in her fingers.

Emily found it hard to sit still. She wondered if they should go look for the men, but as it was almost pitch dark and she had no idea where they were, she dismissed the idea. "Can I get you something...more wine, a cup of tea? The water on the woodstove is hot."

"Tea would be nice. Wish I brought mine now. I could do a reading for you to pass the time."

"You read tea leaves?"

"Oh, yes. My mum taught me years ago."

"There are tea bags in the Ritz," said Emily nodding toward the decrepit structure. "Ben brought a bag of them in case I wanted any."

"Won't do," said Michelle. "Has to be loose tea. I prefer oolong myself. Mum wouldn't use any other kind. Folks that knew her called her a witch you know."

"No," said Emily. "I didn't know. Was she really a witch?"

Michelle chuckled. "An angel would be more apt. Mum had a heart of gold. She was everyone's friend and everyone who knew her loved her too."

Emily sighed loudly. She kicked a loose rock over with her toe and bent to see if any insects were hiding underneath. Nothing. "I'll go make us some tea then. You okay here?"

"I'm fine, darling. And don't worry about your future. Get Ben to bring you to the next Pow Wow with him. He never misses one. I'll have my oolong with me then and I'll give you a good reading. You'll see."

"Sounds like fun. Want anything in your tea?"

"Bourbon would be nice about now. But seeing as how I don't have any, I'll take it black. You can grab some proper mugs out of my trailer."

Michelle went back to fretting with her fringe and Emily left to make the tea. In the few solitary moments she had preparing it, Emily toyed with the notion of working on her story. Maybe she could get a woman's perspective on hunting from Michelle. Tyrone wanted a story that would entice all outdoorsmen. Why not outdoorswomen as well?

Then she deep sixed the idea. It was hopeless to think she could focus on anything other than the man who captured her heart. She brought the tea back to the fire, Ben consuming her every thought.

Chapter Fourteen

Doris flicked the ash from her cigarette and took another drag before looking back through the window. Ava blinked and shuddered under the exertion of propping herself against the woodpile. Her cane was out of reach. She had been trying to nudge the dark staff with the toe of her boot.

"Benny!" she cried out. "Jack! Anybody!"

There was no sign of the weasel, the cause of her predicament. Would Ben's mother be its next meal? The thought of the dark creature slinking towards Ava, ready to sink its teeth into her vulnerable neck, made Doris smile.

Ava winced periodically as if waves of pain were shooting through her body. Suddenly, she stopped rubbing her right leg and twisted forward, rolling onto her stomach. Then she dug in and proceeded to drag herself towards the barn door. It wasn't far.

There's a stubborn old goat. Doris could watch no longer. She stamped out the cigarette, left the window and strode around the corner of the barn. She stood there for a moment, hands on hips, staring down at the teary eyed women. "Got yourself in a bit of a jam do you, Ava?" She stepped over the prone figure, located the cane and picked it up. "How long you been here like this?"

"Too damn long." Ava's breath came in short gasps. "Help me up."

Doris bent and ran her hands down Ava's slight body. "Tell me when you feel pain. Does your back or neck hurt?"

"No. It's my ankle. Must have sprained it when I fell. I was chasing a weasel."

"Were you now?" Doris looked around for a chair or something to sit Ava on while she went for her car. That's when she spied her antique dresser in the corner piled high with boxes and bags.

"I'll be right back, Ava," said Doris, her voice free from expression. "I left my car at ...down the road."

She would have said 'at home' if she hadn't seen that Ben removed the rest of her belongings. For the first time, a jolt of trepidation ran through her. But he would take her back. Doris was going to make sure of that.

She knelt beside the elderly woman and stroked her head, thinly covered in damp silver curls. "Don't you worry now, Ava. I'm going to take good care of you. You'll see."

Doris walked back down the lane to Ben's house. Having no concern for being caught going through his home, she took out her old door key. It worked.

She went to the kitchen, took a crystal tumbler from a cupboard and poured herself two fingers of scotch whiskey from a bottle in the pantry. Savoring the strong, smoky flavor, she strode through the house looking for signs of another woman.

She decided Ben's mother could wait a few more minutes. Ava's injury didn't appear to be life threatening and she felt no urgency in coming to her rescue. Having scouted out the rest of the house, Doris strode into Ben's office and picked up a phone on his desk. Scanning the caller ID list, the name and number of an Emily Paige caught her eye. Now she was getting emotional. She scribbled a note on a red paper napkin, set the glass on top of it and stormed out.

"I'm coming, mother," she muttered. "You haven't seen the last of Doris King, my dear. Not by a long shot." A mordant smile crossed her lips as she gunned down the lane towards the barn. Not really knowing the outcome, her excitement soared. Life was a gamble after all. It could go either way. Though it didn't hurt to know she now had an ace up her sleeve.

When ready she strode into the barn, scooped Ava off the battered floor and deposited her in the front seat of her car. "Home or hospital, Ava?" She would take the old woman wherever she needed to go, for now.

"Home," said Ava. "I need to lay down. And I need some juice. And my nurse. Call Rosie for me. You'll help me won't you?"

"Yes, yes, Ava. I'll help you. We'll help each other." Doris tried to sound sincere, concerned even. What the hell? She reached over and gave the old woman's hand a gentle squeeze. "You've always been like family to me, Ava. What wouldn't I do for you?"

"Thank-you dear. Benny will be so grateful that you were here."

Chapter Fifteen

A beam of bright light broke through the clearing and the tension when Tommy pulled in beside the roaring bonfire. Emily had pulled Michelle out of her seat at the first sound of his engine.

"I told you," sniffled Michelle. "Ben always brings Tommy back to me."

There were tears in her eyes and because of them Emily welled up and started to cry too. Then she realized it was more than that. The relief she felt upon seeing Ben. It shook her to her core, and though she didn't understand where the flood of emotion came from, it didn't matter anymore. She was truly happy to see him.

She ran to Ben and threw her arms around his neck. "Hey...you had me worried."

He hugged her back. "You didn't give me a chance to warn you." He kissed her forehead and broke their embrace just long enough to lead her back to the fire.

When they stepped into the light she saw that the men were soaking wet. Tommy had rushed to comfort Michelle and warm up close to the fire.

"Warn me that you were wet or that your definition of the word 'soon' meant four hours later?" She cast her eyes to the ground. Her words sounded harsh and she hadn't meant them to come out that way. "Not that it makes a difference now."

"Both I guess." Ben shrugged off his soggy overcoat and hung it across a camp chair. "Go have a look."

Emily caught Michelle's nod and followed her to the back of the truck. They looked inside. A cow moose lay on her back spread apart to facilitate the exposure of meat to the cold air.

Tommy spoke up, obviously pleased with their acquisition. "She was dry. Couldn't have bred last season. Only three or four years old. Perfect eating."

Emily put her hand to her mouth and turned away. She didn't want to look at the dead animal anymore. Didn't anyone feel any empathy for these poor creatures? Then she thought about the last hamburger she ate and the life that animal must have led before it ended up on her plate.

She sighed, staring back across the fire at Ben hovering over the flames. She stood there for a moment staring into his smoldering eyes. What was he thinking? She hugged Michelle and said goodnight then went to Ben and took his arm.

"I'm going to put more wood in the woodstove and fill a big rubber tub with hot water," she purred into his ear. "Interested?"

"Sounds like heaven," Ben shivered momentarily, took her hand and spun her towards the Ritz.

"And, by the way," she tossed over her shoulder. "I don't care what the neighbors say behind our backs."

Chapter Sixteen

"Come here, Jack. Come say hello, boy." Doris patted her leg. The hound came towards her, head down, tail wagging timidly between his hind legs.

"He never did like you that much. Did you, Jack?" At the sound of her voice or the mention of his name, Jack perked up and bound over to Ava laying across her divan, a plush pillow supporting her right ankle.

"Do you have to be so blunt all the time?" snarled Doris.

"Yes. It's my nature. Do you have to be so cold all the time?" Ava countered while settling the hound by her side.

"Yes, in fact," through gritted teeth. Then Doris softened her tone. "I mean no. I don't have to be. Now that I know what was wrong with me. Still is, but I'm working on it. That's why I'm back. To tell Ben. It's something I can work out. You'll see."

Ava would have been happy to see Doris leave knowing her nurse was on the way and Doris could sense that intuitively. A span of light drifted through the living room curtains to herald the arrival of Rosie followed by the slam of a car door. Ava spoke before she had time to come in.

"Where are you staying, dear? I have some lovely rhubarb and strawberry jam in the pantry. You'll have to take some with you now, when you go."

Doris rose from a beautifully restored wingback chair and picked up her black leather coat. "Fine. I'll be in touch. Tell Ben I'm staying at the Holiday Inn in Bangor. He has my number."

Rosie came in through the kitchen while Doris lingered at the front door.

The bewildered nurse rushed over to Ava. "What's happened? I near keeled over when I got the call. And who owns that horrid black car outside?"

Doris coughed loudly and Rosie looked up in surprise.

"I'm sorry. I didn't see you there."

Doris ignored her and slipped out the door, leaving enough of a gap that she could hear their conversation and see what Rosie would do next.

"Rosie...do me a favor."

"Anything. What would you have me do now?" She fussed over Ava's ankle, checking the ugly purple bruise and the swelling.

"Next time you're at the drug store pick me up a copy of American Outdoorsman, that magazine my Benny is going to be in."

"But the story isn't even written yet, let alone published."

"I know," said Ava. "I just want to read this girl's work. If she's going to be the mother of my grandchildren, I want to know something about her. As it is I know very little. I don't like that."

"No, you wouldn't would you? Ava, I don't like the looks of this. I'm going to get some witch hazel for the bruising. You need a fresh ice pack as well. Then I'm going to check your blood sugars. How are you feeling?"

The old woman let out a very audible sigh for such a small insignificant figure, thought Doris.

"I feel like the Queen of Scotland with you fussing over me, Rosie. Now be a good girl and go get us a couple of scotch. It's Friday night for God's sake."

Doris quietly shut the door and slunk out of the shadows. An hour later she screeched to a halt outside a Bangor drugstore. She needed to buy a magazine. An ace up her sleeve didn't appear to give much hope after eavesdropping on Ava and her nurse.

Chapter Seventeen

Emily dodged her roommate in their apartment doorway, but Caitlyn blocked her at each attempt to enter. She finally gave up trying to avoid her friend's incredulous stare and dropped her bags.

"What the heck happened to you and where have you been? A cabbie came to the door to take your stuff." Caitlyn's voice strained to an uncomfortably high pitch. "And that's all I know. Talk to me!"

"Okay, get a hold of yourself. And, please let me in the door. You'll wake up the dead!"

Caitlyn took a breath, grabbed Emily's bags and set them down in the hallway leading to their bedrooms.

"Oh my, Cait', I don't know where to begin. Can I grab a soda and relax for a minute? I just drove an hour from Wesley and I'm really tired."

Caitlyn dropped her hands from her hips and sulked into the living room. "Take your time, by all means," she said. "I got all night. In fact, I had the whole weekend to myself while *you* went on vacation."

"It wasn't a holiday. It was work. That's all...I think," she added wistfully.

Emily wasn't sure how much she wanted to share. In truth, she wasn't sure what to tell her about Ben that didn't regard work. He was a world away. Everything happened so fast. It all seemed like a dream.

"He's really nice," she said at last. The charger for her phone lay on a side table where she left it, reminding her to plug in.

Caitlyn had immersed herself in her tablet, but perked up on the heels of a promised story. "Who's nice? Keep going. I want to hear everything. But, first would you look at this. I sent two messages and still no reply from Crane." She handed Emily the tablet and pulled her legs up underneath her on a crimson sofa waiting to be comforted.

Emily peered into the screen then closed the cover and sat down beside her. "You wrote, 'Cat *gut* your tongue?' No wonder he never responded. Probably thinks you're some kind of S and M freak."

"Holy crap! You're kidding!" Caitlyn snatched back the tablet. "I hadn't heard from him since he left for New York for his audition. Thought I wrote 'cat got your tongue?' Jeese, you're right. Now what am I going to do?"

"Tell him the truth, Caitlyn," said Emily shrugging off her sweater. "You're a hopeless illiterate who relies heavily on her roommate, a consummate copyeditor, for proofreading services – who just happened to be away on assignment for a wildly popular lifestyle magazine."

Emily picked through a stack of mail, mostly flyers, on the coffee table while Caitlyn adjusted her legs over the cushions.

"Nothing interesting here. Did you miss me at all?"

"I did." Caitlyn laid her head on Emily's shoulder. "It was lonely here without you. And Crane hadn't messaged me in days. I've stopped eating again."

Emily winced. Caitlyn got to her knees on the sofa, made a halfhearted attempt to rise then collapsed with renewed despair into the overstuffed cushions.

"You poor thing." Emily rose and walked through the kitchen aisle taking in the dirty plates and a bowl left in the sink. She stopped short of checking the oven for dirty pots and pans. It was a given. Instead, she went back to the sofa. Emily put her arms around Caitlyn and began to rock her gently.

Then she pounced. "Nice try! But you forgot to clean the evidence." Emily proceeded to tickle her friend until she dutifully begged for mercy and promised to wash the dishes.

Having freed herself from Emily's torturous fingers, Caitlyn got up and, ignoring the sink, went back to her tablet. "You're too good to me, girlfriend. But since you are, can you make us some of your special popcorn? I'll wash the dishes in a minute. Then you can tell me all about your trip this weekend. I can't wait to hear how the subject of your interview managed to kidnap you. Wine or club soda?"

Not waiting to be answered, Caitlyn went to a kitchen cupboard, took out two wine glasses, and filled them with a South African Shiraz.

A familiar 'plop' brought Emily's attention to her phone. She smiled seeing there was a message from Ben. He signed with x's and o's. "Ben wants to show me his hunting lodge, any time after Wednesday, so I can get some more pictures for my story. And I have more questions for him than ever."

"The kidnapper? Sounds like a date...just sayin'. I'm still waiting to hear about your weekend, whenever you care to enlighten me."

"I'm not sure you want to hear too much about this trip. All that beautiful nature coupled with blood, guts and gore. You wouldn't like it."

"Sounds lovely." Caitlyn drawled. She'd learned the art of sarcasm from the best. "So there's no romantic interest? Too bad. He sure was easy on the eyes." She shrugged. "What do you think of this one? He wants to take me to the corn maze next weekend."

"What about Crane?"

"Crane who?" Caitlyn was studying the screen on her tablet again. She had it opened to MaineMatch.com, a popular on-line dating website. The bright brown eyes of a young man with an olive complexion gazed out of a box on the screen.

"Meet Mohamad."

"You're hopeless!" Emily went to the kitchen and rummaged through a cupboard for the popcorn and seasonings. After placing the items on the black granite breakfast bar, she picked up her stemmed glass and swirled the contents, sniffing bold aromas of spice and plum. "Come on Cait! You *know* I can't work in this mess." She leaned into a nearby stool and took a healthy slurp of the wine.

Caitlyn closed her tablet but kept it in hand as she stepped up to the bar. "I've been reading, you know, about inner peace and all that. Well, one of the suggestions in this self-help book is to catastrophize events surrounding whatever is producing anxiety so as to make it sound absolutely ridiculous. Takes the edge right off. Would you like to try it?"

"In what context?" Emily took another sip of wine. She was quite familiar with the technique herself.

"Well, let's take the dirty dishes. I had been worried about them. All those pathogens lying about...not to mention facing your dish-pleasure!" Emily didn't laugh so she continued. "You just say 'what's the worst that could happen?' and then imagine just that. Are you with me?"

Emily nodded. She was trying to listen, but moments with Ben kept swirling in and out of her head. Caitlyn went on to describe the dire consequences of being unable to keep up with the housekeeping. Her vision, from beginning to end, centered on those dishes and a single bacteria that evolved into a super bug, infecting everyone on the planet, "threatening life as we know it."

Emily grinned, sipped some wine and sagged further into her stool.

Caitlyn downed her glass and set it on the bar. "I hadn't thought of a *worst thing* than you finding them here when you got home."

Emily laughed despite herself. As a friend, she may be a little lazy, but what she lacked in housekeeping, she made up for with heart. Emily leaned over and handed Caitlyn her glass. "Here's one more. I'm going to shower and unpack, while you save the world. Then we'll talk."

Chapter Eighteen

The Wesley farmhouse had been beautifully restored.
Massive oak beams, a floor to ceiling fireplace in angel stone, walls
plastered and painted a creamy white. Ben gazed up at a large tartan
panel that covered one wall in the living room. An apt backdrop for
Ava, sitting poker-straight on her antique divan, her bruised ankle
propped up on a plush velvet pillow. A tiffany lamp cast a pale glow
beside her, softening the sharp cut of her voice as she spun her tale.

"I tried to be nice to her. But then Rosie came by and I didn't
need Doris anymore. She's got some silly notion that she can waltz
back into your life like nothing happened." Ava picked up the
magazine beside her and flipped it open. "This Emily girl is talented
and quite pretty I must say. I've been reading some of her work.
What do you think of her?"

Think of her? Since she left his home Sunday evening, Ben
could think of little else. Except, the red light flashing on his phone
when they returned to civilization needled him. Then he saw the
slight trail of sawdust sweeping across the floor towards his office
and his heart skipped a beat.

He was almost relieved when Emily left for Bangor. She'd
been eager to get home and finish a story so that she could give her
full attention to the hunting issue. He'd drawn her close. Smoky
remnants clung to red-tinged curls. They parted haltingly. A gentle
kiss, a hug, a wave goodbye. And she was gone. As if they had

parted a thousand times before, a level of comfort knowing they would be together again – soon.

"Benny!"

"Sorry. What was that?" Ben dabbed a liniment soaked cloth on Ava's wounded leg. "You said something about Doris."

"I said little about Doris. It's Emily I want to talk to you about. What's she like? Where does she live? Have you met her family?"

What's she like? "She's like a breath of fresh mountain air. She's kind and funny, daring yet domestic. She's got class, sass and the most gorgeous...smile."

That comment earned Ben a cuff on the top of the head. He chuckled and continued. "She has the voice of an angel and the grace of a deer. Ambitious too. She'll go far," he sighed and stood to stretch a cramp in his leg. "How's that? Better?"

"Much. Thank-you. Now what are you going to do about Doris? As much as I hate to bring her up again, it looks like she's here to win you back. Not that I think you'll give in to her after all this time, but I have a feeling she's not going to go quietly."

"She won't have a choice. I talked with her this morning. She's coming to get the rest of her things tomorrow. Then she's going back to Presque Isle. Not much chance for her to raise havoc from three hours away."

"Don't kid yourself," Ava said dryly. "Doris can't resist a challenge."

The proof of that statement lay atop the cold hearth in Ben's fireplace. After Emily left, he discovered an empty crystal tumbler and a note on red paper with Doris's unmistakable penmanship, thanking him for the nightcap. She'd left them on the desk beside the phone in his office. He'd gone to the fireplace, crumpled the paper and tossed it inside, fighting an urge to hurl the glass in as well. Then he dropped it on the mantel and fled out the door.

Rosie tried to stop Ben from charging inside his mother's house. She had only come around to the front when he literally ran into her, knocking the car keys out of her hand. She gave him the short version, for she wasn't there to see it all, and convinced him that Doris had not been around since Friday afternoon.

Ava, she insisted, was healing well and would be back to her old self in no time. But she wasn't there yet. "I just got her medicated, comfortable and shut up, Mr. Blackheart. Can't you come back in the morning?"

The shake of his head and the fear in his eyes told her no. Rosie stood firm. "Stubborn lot. You come by it honestly enough. Go on then. But make it brief. She needs her rest." She took her keys from Ben and thanked him for picking them up.

"Thank-you, Rosie." He kissed her cheek and ran inside.

Seeing Ava prone, her breath rhythmic and slow, as in a deep sleep, Ben decided her story could wait until morning. He pulled an heirloom quilt up over her svelte shoulders, softly stroked the soft fluff of silver laying on a crisp white pillowcase and left. What could have happened? Anything, was the immediate answer and the horror of that realization made him shudder.

Outside, a whimper from Jack had snapped him out of dire contemplation. "Let's go home, boy. Heaven knows what tomorrow will bring."

Jack now sprawled at his master's feet. Ben sat in the wingback. His gaze never left Ava as he patted the hound's head and smoothed his fur.

"What else can I do for her? She doesn't need me. She hasn't asked for anything either. That's the part that scares me. She'd never been one to...to settle." The closest he could think to describe her in one sentence. At the moment, it seemed to fit Doris to a tee.

Ava scowled. "Someone should keep an eye on her then. She did say she was working on something, but I was only half listening. Perhaps I should have paid closer attention."

"Pay no attention, mother. If you hadn't mentioned my being off with another woman, she might not have bothered to come round at all." Ben scowled now, incensed by the thought of Doris knowing his personal affairs.

"Well, I didn't know it would become more than a business venture when I told her a reporter had gone with you to the Highlands. Has it?" she asked.

"Become more than a business venture, you mean?"

"Yes, that is the burning question."

"Oh."

"Oh, my." Ava smiled. It acknowledged that she understood more than what he meant to imply.

Ben bristled. "She may have let it go if you hadn't mentioned Michelle going there as well. Made it sound like a couple's thing."

Ava pulled a creamy handmade afghan over her lap and smoothed the wool down over her legs. "Was it...a couple's thing?"

Ben thought about that. Emily didn't know his friends existed when she agreed to go with him. The only reason Michelle had come was because Tommy begged her and promised the companionship of another woman. Emily had come because she needed a story, she needed him – but there was more. She wanted to please him. He felt it the moment she looked into his pleading eyes and took his hand.

"I guess it was. Mother?"

"Yes, Benny?"

"If she calls again. Doris. Don't tell her anything. From now on, my life is none of her business. Okay?"

Ava bobbed her head and smiled. "Yes, Benny. I won't answer the phone when she calls next time."

"I hope there is no next time. I want to get on with my life. And take care of you. I'll be taking a break now that the Grafton design is off my plate. I can work from home until summer when you go to Uncle John's for your vacation. Apparently, you can't be trusted by yourself anymore."

"Just a minute," Ava started to grumble, but Ben's glare stilled her.

"I'm not going to let anything happen to you, mother. Get used to it."

"I'm used to it already. You're all like bloody hawks watching over me all the time."

"That's only because I love you, mom. Uncle John loves you, your friends and Rosie and don't forget Jack."

The hound stretched on his side at the sound of his name and yawned so long and hard his jaws appeared to separate and fall apart, though they snapped together again after a moment.

"Besides, what in the name of blazes did you think you were going to do with a weasel if you caught one anyway? Thump it on the head with your cane?"

"Precisely what I thought to do. But my cane was too heavy. I need a lighter one, Benny. Maybe you can whittle me one out of a bit of pine."

Ben glanced at her in mock annoyance. "Not a chance, mother. Not a bloody chance."

Chapter Nineteen

Doris had one appointment in Bangor. She left the psychiatric unit of the women's medical building with a new prescription and renewed hope. The lapse in time could be forgiven. She'd done nothing wrong. Yet.

But now here she was, and the only man she'd ever loved wanted her things out of his house. What was left? Some of the Christmas presents Ben had given her were left behind. A pile of favored magazines, some animal carvings, a duvet. She'd kept the gold and amethyst ring he'd given her. That, she lost in a poker game one month later, on the reservation in Presque Isle. Too bad. It was a pretty ring.

She didn't miss it, though she should have. Ben noticed her bare finger when she returned home from a three-week conference. She'd lied and told him she lost it down the drain in her hotel bathroom.

She accused him of buying the wrong size, putting the blame for its demise on his shoulders. Ben didn't say anything, but she knew he was furious. He'd left the house in a huff with a Winchester slung over his shoulder.

That's when she wrote the *Dear Ben* letter and left it on his pillow. She was angry when he didn't come after her. She felt vindicated when Donald, Ben's father, died. Why should she be the only one to suffer? But then she spoke with Ava. Ben, off with another woman. That tidbit of information infuriated her.

Doris jumped in her car and dodged into morning traffic. She hit the open road to Wesley and gunned the engine. Willing the tires to stay locked on pavement, she streaked through the countryside taking turns at breakneck speeds. Life on the edge – the unknown elements – now she felt alive!

Grinding to a crawl, her pulse slowed. She nudged the car down Ben's private lane dwelling on what she had to tell him. Would he be shocked? What would he do?

It should go favorably, thanks to Ava. He'd probably fall all over himself thanking her for saving his precious mother. She allowed herself a thin smile. He'd be ever so courteous then. Take her coat, offer her a drink, crush her in his arms...then all would be forgiven. Hell, she'd bet her own mother on that.

Chapter Twenty

Emily turned in *Hallowed Hikers* on schedule Monday morning. She'd been up half the night working on edits, the stillness and constant hum of the apartment building her only distractions. No cheeping tree frogs, no bird songs, no coyote howls to steal a moment from the task at hand. No Ben.

Shortly after leaving her office the electrician met with her on Oak Boulevard. She was pleased to learn that necessary upgrades to the electrical panel wouldn't put her in the poor house. She meant that in the most literal of terms. Now she could afford to buy the wood she needed to finish replacing the bathroom floor. If the gods kept smiling on her, she could start picking out paint colors by the end of the week.

Today was Thursday. Ben, having whatever business he'd had to attend to out of the way, expected her to return for a visit to the hunting lodge. She decided to work at her downtown cubical. It would be a closer drive to Wesley come day's end. She immersed herself in the hunting issue. Working in fits of release produced some compelling work, but the simplest annoyance became monumental, squeezing her creative juices dry. Where was all this stress coming from?

Another pencil cracked under pressure. The rubber end stuck in her pearly white teeth. It didn't help that she caused most of those annoyances herself. If only she could stop thinking about Ben.

He'd had loads of time to think about her. How silly she behaved at times. How horrid she must have looked in the morning waking up next to him. Did she snore too? Caitlyn had accused her of it more than once, usually after a night of overindulgence, but still. And he knew she was struggling, still trying to reach a comfortable level of success. How could she have made love with him that night, and the next, as if nothing else mattered?

At the time nothing else did. Each time he took her in his arms he'd become more demanding, more insistent on drawing out her pleasure, denying his release until her thirst was fully quenched. Only then, spurred by her ecstatic moans and sudden moistness, would he climax. He promised to satisfy every carnal desire she'd ever had.

It was a nice thought. Not that she believed him. Although he did seem to be really into me, she mused, then grinned at her pun. Emily wanted to be more than just a plaything to Ben. A plaything. How else could he possibly see her? The thought hung over her like a dark cloud.

Thunk! She torpedoed the broken pencil into a tin trashcan under her desk and checked the wall clock for the fiftieth time that day.

Time to go.

She opened her desk drawer, took out a new package of batteries for her camera and threw them in her slouch purse. When she reached the end of the cubicle-lined hallway, Tyrone opened his office door and gave her a nod that said, "Inside, now!"

Ambushed. How long is this going to take? She swallowed hard, then followed her boss through the heavy oak door.

"*Hallowed Hikers.*" Tyrone held the manuscript in hand as he pushed a ceramic picture frame out of his way and hung a cheek on the edge of his desk.

"Is everything okay?" Emily stood near the door to facilitate a quick escape.

"You look nervous. Is everything okay with you?" Tyrone placed both hands behind him on the massive piece of teak furniture that dominated the room.

"I was thinking about the story. I really tried to do a good job. Did you find it lame?"

Tyrone snorted and laughed. "You're a 'punny' girl, Emily. I think that's why your stories are so delightful. Your wit, your style, the way you draw pictures with words and let the reader draw his or her own conclusions, brilliantly manipulated by evoking feelings for the characters in your stories. You're a real charmer. I'd like you to keep it up."

"Well, thank-you. I'll do my best. I really do like working for the magazine. Is that all?" It was all she could do to keep her hands off his solid brass doorknob.

"Not quite." Tyrone flicked a bit of lint from the razor sharp crease of his pant leg, paused to admire his manicure, then stood. "I have a mind to nominate you for a literary award." He picked up her manuscript and waved it in the air. "This is good, very good, but it isn't a full showcase of your talent. I have a feeling your next story is going to be the kicker. I can't wait to lay eyes on it." He tossed thirty-five hundred words back on his desk accompanied by a look of exasperation. "Okay, run along. You've kept your beau waiting long enough. Lord knows you've accomplished nothing here today."

"I'm really sorry about the…"

"Out!"

He didn't have to tell her again.

Chapter Twenty-one

Ben lit the candles when he heard Emily's car drive into his yard. He'd prepared a light supper – wild mushroom soup and a green salad. The table had been set. A bottle of red wine left to breathe on the counter. A timid knock came from outside.

"Come in!" Ben wondered if he'd absentmindedly locked the door. It was a habit he'd never developed. By God, she should be in by now. He went to the door, flung it open. Emily stood on the veranda, baguette in hand.

Freshly baked from the local market guessed Ben. A delicious aroma wafted from the tip of a long brown paper bag. "Smells wonderful. Good enough to eat."

"You're talking about this, correct?" She waved the stick of bread at him like a pirate brandishing a sword.

"Get in here wench," he said. "I'm talking about you. Nothing else comes close to satisfying my hunger." He took the baguette and tossed it on a nearby sideboard, then he took her in his arms. "Kiss me. Now," he demanded.

Her arms trailed up to his neck and pulled him closer. "Like this?"

Her kiss set him on fire. He pulled away, a searing heat rising in his loins.

"Stay with me tonight." His throat tightened. "I want you. Tell me you'll stay." Then he kissed her back, eager to unleash his passion.

"I don't know how to say no to that." Emily wavered when he released her, breath coming in quick short gasps.

Quite pleased with himself, or at least with the effect he had on Emily, Ben eased her into a rattan chair, then gently pulled off her green rubber boots.

"For our jaunt to the hunting lodge. I didn't imagine you'd have a paved road leading up to it. And it's not going to get any warmer before spring," she said in explanation. "I didn't take the moccasins home that you gave me, but if they're around now I'll put them on. My feet get cold easily."

"Of course." Ben opened a closet door beside the sideboard and took out the slippers. "I like that you feel comfortable enough to leave some of your things here. There's only one washroom so we'll have to share, but you get your own toothbrush, and I bought fresh towels and linens when I went shopping this week. I want you to feel comfortable when you're with me."

As he knelt to take Emily's foot, he was surprised to see moist amber spots inside the moccasins. They lay in the soft fur lining. He sniffed the one in his hand. Maple syrup?

"What is it?" Emily hadn't seen the drops yet, but from her tone, she knew something was wrong.

"I'll get you a pair of wool socks. They'll be much warmer. Be right back." He reached down to pick up the other slipper, but Emily snatched it off the floor before him.

"What's this?"

"Maple syrup. It will wash out." He held out his hand for the soiled slipper.

Ben coaxed her to follow him into his bedroom. She sat on the bed while he went to a sturdy, Quaker-style dresser.

"Who would do such a thing?"

It was a fair question. "I guess I haven't told you much about Doris."

Emily frowned. "I don't believe you mentioned her, no." She scanned the room for signs of her presence – a photograph, a feminine piece of clothing, a stray hair on his pillows – nothing. "You are single, aren't you?"

"Absolutely. Here put these on. I'm going to pour us some wine. And first thing in the morning, I'm calling a locksmith."

Emily thought it strange that he hadn't gotten around to changing his locks almost a year after the dissolution of a relationship, but she didn't say anything. Michelle had mentioned Ben's former girlfriend in passing, as if she were ancient history. She snugged the warm wool around her ankles and went to join Ben in the kitchen. She hoped history wouldn't be around to repeat itself.

They began their aromatic meal in relative quiet. That is, until the slurping of soup and Emily's exaggerated moans of delight dissolved into laughter.

"Sounds like you're having a climax in your mouth," chuckled Ben. "I'm not that good a chef am I?"

"I'm reserving judgment. Maybe we should go back to your room and see what else we can cook up."

"Heed my warning. I'm having you for desert."

Much later, she lay naked across Ben's back tracing a finger over a faded scar on his right shoulder. "Hunting accident?" she pried.

"You could call it that," he said cautiously.

"Well, it looks like you were stabbed in the back, and I can't think of any circumstance that would have brought that on you, so it must have been an accident. Unless you have a better explanation." She kissed the scar, then slid onto the sheets, herself and them still damp from lustful exertions.

Ben rolled on his side to face her. "I didn't exactly tell you the truth about how I met Tommy."

Emily raised up on one elbow and caressed his face with her free hand. "You want to tell me now?"

"It's a long story."

"I'm committed for the night. Unless you've changed your mind. I can still get dressed and go home."

She made the slightest gesture to rise before Ben grabbed her wrist and held on. "You're not going anywhere at this time of night." He lay on his back then and pulled her down so that her head lay in the crook of his arm, one hand holding hers on top of his broad chest.

The story he told was nothing she could have imagined. It began twenty years ago when Americans were still fighting communism in El Salvador and Nicaragua. He'd been recruited – not regular army. It was for the militia, guns for hire. The lure of fast money got to him. He needed it for tuition, and for the house he wanted to build for himself.

Only it wasn't his shooting skills they'd been after. Least not with a gun. He was Special Forces, chosen for his skill with the crossbow, same as Tommy. That's how they met. In a war torn jungle. Somehow they kept each other alive and made it home with bankrolls large enough to finance their immediate needs.

Emily nuzzled into Ben, savoring the warmth of his skin, conscious of a threatening chill as the perspiration dried on her skin. He felt her slight shudder and pulled the bedding up over her shoulders, pulled her closer and kissed her forehead.

"Did you have a girlfriend back then? I can't imagine having my man go through those extremes just to make a few dollars." Emily consciously relaxed in his hold, not wanting him to sense the discomfort she felt in asking. Did she really want to remind him of a past love? Yes, she wanted to know – had to know – what made this man tick. And the time to deny she had fallen in love had run out.

Ben chuckled. "It was more than a few dollars. I was twenty years old with thirty-five thousand dollars in my pocket. At the time, I felt like a millionaire."

Ben unlocked his grip and moved to his side. She met his gaze and deliberately relaxed in a most submissive pose the hitch in his throat was audible. He took a deep cleansing breath, then poured out his soul like dark, warm chocolate.

"El Salvador – home to the most beautiful women in the world. And they don't even know that they're women." He grimaced at a distant memory. "They rose each morning and put on automatic weapons and hand grenades...like American women put on jewelry and make up."

Ben inched his fingers along a smooth silver chain that hung from Emily's neck. He caressed her cheek. Then he slid his hand down the chain to the small turquoise stone hidden in the fold of her breast. He tugged. Soon, she felt the warmth of his breath on her lips. She was breathless. He bent and kissed her, with more passion than she'd ever experienced. When he let go of the thin chain that bind them together their lips parted, leaving her weak.

"You poor thing, what you must have gone through," she whispered.

Chapter Twenty-two

There's something unsettling about waking up in the morning with a new lover. If they're not awake, you don't want to disturb them. If they are awake, what are they doing? Trying not to disturb you? Emily cracked a lid. "Have you been watching me sleep?"

He kissed the tip of her nose. "It's still cold. But your feet are warm."

Emily became aware of her legs, tangled in his under the bedding. "Cold nose, warm heart."

Woof!

"What was that?"

"Jack," said Ben pulling away. He grabbed a housecoat from a hook behind the bedroom door. "Mother must be up. I sent him to stay with her last night."

Ben left to let him in while Emily scanned the room for something warm to slip on. She found a soft cotton shirt in the closet and was buttoning it down when an exuberant Bluetick hound scampered into the room.

"Hi, Jack." Emily dropped to the floor. Jack went to her, tail wagging, tongue licking, and nose nosing in where it didn't belong.

"What will it be this morning?" Ben called from the kitchen. "I have Columbian, Sumatra and a Kenya blend. And, I haven't a clue what to do with either of them."

Jack led Emily to the kitchen. She stopped in the doorway. Ben looked adorable, scratching his head and rubbing his chin. His hair was disheveled and stubble tinged his jawline. The stubble added an extra degree of masculinity, if that were possible. A long black robe exposed tawny skin and muscle.

He could play Tarzan to my Jane any day, she thought wistfully. Ben was solitary, but not unsocial...reserved, but certainly not cold. She admired his independence. Liked the way he made her feel – useful. *I get what I need.* A man like Ben could have anything – anyone, he wanted. Could she even hope to believe that he wanted her?

Emily slipped her arms around the curve in his back when he opened his robe to draw her in. "Sumatra is wonderful. I'll make it."

"I was hoping you'd say that." He gave her an appreciative kiss on the forehead before getting shooed away.

"Go sit down. Jack needs your attention too."

Emily prepared the coffee maker using precise measurements from the back of the gold foil package. "Now what can we do while this is brewing?"

"Come here and I'll show you." Ben opened his robe to draw her in again.

A knock on the front door stopped her short. Feeling overexposed, wearing nothing but a shirt and wool socks, Emily fled to the bedroom. She picked up her maroon turtleneck and dark brown Chinos, a rumpled mess on the dusty bamboo floor, and shook them out. Could use a woman's touch, she thought absentmindedly.

The voice of an older woman inside the house suddenly filled her with dread and shame. What would his mother think of her spending the night with her son?

She never had the chance to test that equation on her own parents, but she knew their approval would be hard won, if at all. Sex was a gift that two people shared after an exchange of vows. The kind that meant forever. There was no loophole in place to condone casual encounters. She dressed, then sat on the edge of the bed.

Ben came in to shrug on a pair of jeans and grab a T-shirt. When he noticed Emily's lost expression and misty eyes, he knelt at her feet.

"What's wrong?" There was pain in his voice, as if he felt her discomfort. "I want you to meet my mother. She's dying to meet *you*. Can you smile for me?" His voice was sincere, cajoling and full of hope.

Emily managed a slight grin. "I have to freshen up before I meet your mom. Can you get my purse in the foyer and bring it to the bathroom? I just need a minute or two."

"Of course." He kissed the tip of her nose and left to carry out her request.

Ava sat at the kitchen table stirring her coffee. She pushed the small pitcher of cream out of her way and picked up her cup with both hands.

Assessing her son through a pair of small, oval glasses perched on the end of a petite nose, she took a cautious sip.

"Mmm, this is lovely. You should have told me you were out of maple syrup though, Benny. I still have a quart or two in my pantry. You'll have to come get some."

Ben shook his head and raised his own mug to his lips, stopping to savor the aroma before taking a drink. "You've scarcely enough to get you through the winter. I'll be sure to double my efforts next year. It never seems to go far enough. So tell me...how much have *you* given away?" he admonished.

"Not much. A few quarts maybe. I'm afraid I've got Rosie hooked on the stuff. Thankfully she only drinks coffee in the morning, and never more than a cup. She says it's not good for me. Remind me again why I let you saddle me with her. You know I can't stand being told what to do."

"You're sidetracking, mother. So, Rosie is the only person you gave any to at all...you're sure?"

"Of course, I'm sure. I still have all my faculties, whether you think so or not. I've never needed anyone to tell me my own mind."

"Precisely, mother. And that's exactly why Rosie is such a godsend. She doesn't let you have your own way all the time. When it comes down to the important things, you listen to her. That may not be vital to you, but for me it brings peace of mind."

"Which is the only reason I do listen to her," Ava conceded, a hint of indignation in her voice. Her soft grey eyes fluttered momentarily.

Emily took a halting step inside the door frame. "Hello, Mrs. Blackheart. It's so nice to meet you." She cleared the small space between them and took the diminutive and thinly veined hand that Ava extended. She meant only to give it a gentle shake and let go, but Ava held firm and turned in her seat casting her eyes up and down.

"So you're Emily Paige. Childbearing hips I see. That's a good sign." Startled, Emily gaped at the woman on the end of her hand. "Call me Ava, please. I don't like being addressed like an old woman. I've plenty of life in me yet."

Ben rolled his eyes at his mother, then came to Emily's rescue. He held a chair out for her inside the table by a sunny window. "Don't mind her audacity, darling. She's senile and doesn't know any better."

Ava produced a near genuine pout that made Ben chuckle. Emily grinned. The matriarch pressed on. "You look younger in person, dear. I saw your picture in that magazine you work for. I like the way you write too, though the content is not all that appealing to me. I expect that will change when I see Benny's name and face on the pages."

Emily composed herself and said, "thank you, Ava." She kept an eye on Ben as he popped bread in the toaster and cracked eggs into a large glass bowl. "I'm hoping to do him proud."

"I'm sure you will, dear. Well, I didn't come to interrupt your breakfast and I don't want to keep Francine waiting, so I'll take my leave. You two have fun." She stood then, with little effort, though she reached for her cane before taking a step.

"Mother, why don't you let me drive you? The scrambled eggs will be ready in a minute and then…"

"I'm quite capable of driving myself. If I can walk up and down stairs I can drive a car. I drove here didn't I?" Her defiant interruption left no room for discussion. "Besides, Francine will be there to help me when I reach the bingo hall."

"Fine. I'll just walk you out to your car. Emily can you stir the eggs?"

"No problem. Good bye, Ava. It was nice to meet you."

"The pleasure was all mine, dear. I do hope you'll come again."

"I'll certainly try," said Emily.

Ava grinned ear to ear as she left the kitchen while Emily turned three shades of crimson.

"You'll try?"

"I couldn't help it." Emily was quite unable to suppress a torrent of giggles while stirring the eggs, now solidified in a cast iron frying pan.

Ben switched off the gas burner. "Go ahead…laugh. I think she deserved it. Or asked for it, which is worse." He helped himself to a glob of eggs, fluffy and rich with a slight crust on the bottom.

"I think she's a darling, darling." Not quite a Freudian slip, but the endearment came out as a surprise to Emily.

"Darling?"

"You said it first."

"You're so...so right." He broke off a piece of egg with his fingers and popped it between the swell of her lips. "Emily?"

"Yes?"

"I think...." He slipped behind, pulled her hair over one shoulder and kissed the back of her neck. Tingles ran down her spine producing a low moan. He bit down, exerting just enough pressure to elicit another, much louder. He'd hit the sweet spot. Heat rose in her taut body as he pressed in. He trailed a series of light kisses the length of her neck. Emily went limp. Ben caught and tossed her over his shoulder before heading back to the bedroom.

"I think I like terms of endearment. I never did before, but coming from you, I could get used to it." Then he gave her a playful swat on the behind and laid her on the bed. "That was for being a saucy girl. And don't ever stop."

Chapter Twenty-three

A full hour went by before the two lovers were dressed and ready to go to the hunting lodge. They walked to a shed behind the house. Ben went inside to bring out his all-terrain vehicle. It was a yellow Polaris Sportsman 800, the best American-built muscle for woodsmen in production, according to Ben.

Just like a boy, proud of his toys, thought Emily as they bounced through the woods on trails barely distinguishable to her, but apparently well-worn paths to her ruggedly handsome driver. He barreled through meadows, then trundled over small trees and under massive felled trunks when the going got rough. Two miles into the woods they came to a log cabin in a small clearing.

"I'm really glad you asked me to stay over. The light is so much better now than it would have been last evening."

Ben opened the latch on a storage container and passed Emily her camera. He was wearing full regalia now, camouflage pants and jacket, hunting boots and cap. He'd brought four of his favorite rifles: a Kimber, a Remington and two Winchesters.

From outside, the cabin looked as rustic as they come. From the ground up, the logs were sagging and moss covered, while murky windows looked to be impenetrable. A stovepipe listed at an angle behind a peak in the roof, its rusty metal cap holding tenuously to a snarl of wire.

The door hinges were rust colored as well and they squeaked as one would expect when Ben opened the door. He secured it open with a nail, allowing light to flood in and the musty odor to escape. Emily expected the interior of the cabin to be in a similar state of disrepair, but that was not the case.

A primitive kitchen occupied the corner to her right. It lacked appliances but was equipped with a dull stainless steel counter and sink. The cupboards as well as the floor were made of wide planked pine. Door handles were fashioned from small tines of deer antler as were the handles on the push-out, wooden framed windows.

Two sofas with sturdy, canvas-covered cushions provided seating to the left of the door. They were angled towards each other separated by a large, smoked-glass table. Moose antlers, stained in warm dark caramel and varnished, formed the base of the table.

One end of the cabin housed a room with two full-sized plywood bunks. Across from the bedroom door in the opposite corner, stood a chrome dinette ensemble. A large cast iron woodstove, with stainless steel embellishments, dominated the center of the lodge. The quintessential woodsman hangout, thought Emily.

Then, looking up, she gasped. Antlers, deer sculls and long knobby jaws filled the rafters. They only came into view when her eyes adjusted to the dim light. She rubbed her neck and gazed back at Ben after counting more than thirty sets of antlers, most of them fully intact.

"It's quite the collection. How long did it take you to..." the words stuck in her throat.

Ben caught her arm and began to pull her back outside. "You don't have to do this. I didn't realize how frightening it would look. You're a city girl after all? I'm afraid I expected too much of you. Let's go." His voice was tight, his face grim. He tugged on her arm again.

Emily pulled away. "No. I want to stay. I can do this." She took the Canon out of its case. "Talk to me, Ben."

Down to business. *Focus Emily.* She shook off all preconceptions. "This handiwork all yours? Yours...and your father's, I see."

She stopped snapping pictures to stare at a photograph on the wall. Ben was much younger. He and Donald stood over a large buck that lay in the snow, its rack an impressive twelve pointer. She snapped a picture of that as well, and others that hung randomly throughout the cabin.

"This was home for some time. I bought the land and started stripping logs as soon as I returned from El Salvador. Never did bring in running water. There is a well." he scanned the rafters, chose a rare eleven point rack and brought it down. "Dad bagged this one just last year." His voice didn't crack, surprising him. Until then, he hadn't been able to think about his father without emotion kicking him in the gut. "He taught me...everything."

"Keep talking, Ben. Tell me what it's like to be a hunter. What does it feels like to have this kind of power? What's the draw? Is it simply a means of obtaining food or is there something deeper, something primordial beneath it all? I want to know everything." Emily focused on the glass table. It was magnificent. Flash!

"I've sold nine to date. People pay good money for them, up to a thousand dollars." Ben popped open a window letting more sunlight pour in. "The money came in handy when I was starting out in my business. Prototypes are expensive to produce."

"That's another story," she said. "Stay with me, Ben."

"I'll certainly try." He slumped into a vinyl covered seat beside the kitchen table, picked up his Remington and squinted into the scope, pointing the barrel towards the open door.

"Hold it!" Emily snapped the picture. "Can we bring some of these antlers outside, set up some shots around the outside of the cabin?"

"You're the boss." He put down his rifle and went to her. He'd gone long enough without kissing those soft pouty lips.

"You made that sound like a term of endearment."

"It was. Now if you want to get anything else out of me you'll have to kiss me."

"Now who's being bossy?"

"Miss Paige, I believe you've met your match."

"I'd like to think so," she whispered. Then she let him have his way. Work could wait a minute.

Sunday evening came much too soon. By the end of the weekend, Emily felt as though her heart had gone from zero to sixty. She was in love. Leaning into him now on the veranda as they said good bye, she savored the traces of musk and pine that clung to Ben's clothing.

"I love the way your curves melt into me when we cuddle. You fit me so well. When you woke in my arms this morning, I couldn't tell where you left off and I began. It felt like we were one." Ben grew quiet then and there was a long empty pause before he pulled away from their embrace. "I don't know when I'll be able to see you again. I have a few things that I have to take care of." He paused again and Emily knew that he had noticed the sudden hitch in her breathing.

"But it won't be weeks or anything."

She detected a trace of anguish in his voice. Something in his eyes, far more discerning, told Emily that Ben was torn. By what she had no idea. She wasn't even sure if she wanted to know. A shiver went through her. Ben snugged the collar of her coat around her slender neck and drew her to him for a final hug.

"I'll call you."

"Thank-you. For the weekend, for everything." She kissed him good-bye.

Chapter Twenty-four

Ben was true to his word and called to invite her over by Thursday evening. Emily, it turned out, was grateful to have had the time alone. The work week had gone by with few distractions allowing her to become fully absorbed in the hunting story. Now that it was Friday, she would soon be in his arms.

Before leaving the apartment to work at her office cubicle, she packed a bag. She put in a slinky, silk negligee herself this time, and little else. She didn't need much when she was with Ben. Then she remembered Ava and added a long terry robe to her arsenal of seduction. Just in case. Too personal – she took it out.

I like that you feel comfortable enough to leave some of your things here. She stuffed the robe in her travel bag again. Perhaps she would leave it there.

Sitting in her cubicle, she critically analyzed her cache of photographs – Joey with his haughty grin leaning over his first kill, Justine and Patch looking up, their dark slanting eyes awash with adoration. Click, click, click.

She had taken more than a hundred pictures. The cabin, the antlers, the full hunting regalia – Ben. She wondered briefly why she hadn't seen a crossbow. Not one, though in her mind he had more than enough guns. Perhaps the memories were too painful. She clicked on a photo of him in the forest, midstride, a Remington rifle slung over his shoulder.

He'd been walking in front of her through a path near the hunting lodge. Twenty years of trampling kept the ground smooth and hard. The late morning sun streamed over him, illuminating the leaf strewn path ahead. A perfect day lay ahead for one, while the end of life lay in wait for another, she mused. But not that day.

Ben hadn't brought ammunition. Most often, especially since his father died, he hunted alone. Sign was everywhere, though Emily still couldn't distinguish clearly between the pellets of a deer and those of a rabbit. The long, raw scrapes in the bark of trees, he explained, came from deer rubbing their antlers. Other bare patches of wood indicated the presence of porcupine.

She clicked on the photo of an eight-point deer. Ben spotted him first on their way back from the cabin. He was beautiful. A statuesque figure, large brown orbs, staring at them, adrenaline straining to take rise. They had almost driven past him coming out of the woodlot.

The ride was slow and deliberate, the bumps and grinds making Emily damp with arousal. "I could get used to this," she'd moaned in his ear.

He'd stopped suddenly. She guessed he wanted to kiss her, really make her moan. But then, she saw the deer he pointed at in a clearing near the trail. He didn't want her to miss the opportunity. Luckily, Emily kept her camera in hand, clutching onto Ben with her thighs tight to his waist as they clambered over heaving roots and deep ruts in the terrain. After she snapped his picture, the deer vanished.

Emily chose a dozen of her favorite shots and put them in a separate folder on her desktop. She closed the screen, thinking to take a short break for lunch. Her eyes were heavy, her tummy light, a condition brought on by single-minded absorption in her work.

The Hungry Owl was just around the corner and she'd barely spoken to Caitlyn all week.

Emily noted her friend's wary expression when she came into the café and placed her order.

"Cucumber and tomato with light cream cheese on sourdough. And V-8 juice? You feeling ok?"

"Never better." Though she was beginning to feel impatient.

"Okay, but this is the first time in four months that you didn't order egg salad and Sumatra for lunch. What's up?"

"Nothing. I just don't want to taste like raw onions and coffee when I see Ben today. And, I think I'm putting on weight again. My new jeans feel tight already. Can't have that."

"You haven't been running have you?"

"No time."

"Still, all that sex-er-size on the weekends. You're probably imagining the weight gain. I don't see a difference."

"Hush your mouth. The customers will hear." Emily glanced around the room, her gaze settling on an earring studded face and a head sporting short, spiky hair tinged purple at the tips. He was reading a Marvel comic book at her favorite table. She cocked her head to the side. "Isn't that Crane?"

"Right. By the way, you're going for the full weekend aren't you? I told him he could stay with me. We're going to spend the whole time in bed doing the wild thing. I'm not letting him get away this time."

Emily rolled her eyes. "I'll call before I come home."

"Taking this with you or eating in?" Caitlyn sprinkled salt and pepper on top of the tomatoes without asking and finished making the sandwich.

"Bag it please, Cait," said Emily. "I want to finish up early at the office so I can get out of town before the weekend traffic gets gnarly." She paid for her meal and left feeling somewhat dejected.

She missed spending time with her friend. Something that wouldn't be happening if Ben hadn't come along and flipped her world on end. Then again, Crane was back in the picture and she had to admit, he was a perfect match for her quirky friend. They'd naturally be spending less time together, making her appreciate her time with Ben even more.

The afternoon went quickly enough. She'd gotten out of the city before rush hour and was making good time driving towards Wesley. She felt a pang of guilt as she turned up the service road that led to Ben's property. She should be heading to Oak Boulevard to work on renovations. But after his call, saying that he and Jack both missed her, she'd made up her mind to take the weekend off. The way Emily saw it, self-sufficiency came first, then she'd find a husband, have children – three at least – then pets, one at least.

In a moment Jack came barreling down the lane towards her. He now recognized the sound of the Colt's engine. Dear Jack, loyal and trusting, playful and affectionate – varying shades of grey in his soft coat, squared jawline and angular face. Funny how dogs seem to personify their masters, or was it the other way around?

She was still thinking about Ben and the changes that jostled her routine life, when a call came in on her mobile phone, a private number according to her display screen. Ben's contact information was public. She wondered who it could be, but let the call go to voicemail while she pulled in beside Ben's Jeep.

He came outside, bright-eyed and smiling. Emily didn't return his smile. She stared down at her phone screen reading the message that had been transcribed into text and left in her messenger box.

I just left Ben and he was crying.
We'd been to visit his father's grave
and he was really upset.
Take care of him for me. Doris.

Emily knew Donald was buried on Ava's property under a giant oak tree. It stood sentinel on the edge of a grassy meadow overlooking the grand farmhouse. Ben had passed by the gravesite and pointed it out on the way back from his hunting lodge the previous week. They stopped briefly for Ben to adjust a hawthorn wreath he'd made himself and left on a black granite tombstone.

"Dad wasn't into flowers," he'd said with emotion, "unless they were wild." Then they left and his mood instantly brightened. He raced her across the meadow and down the lane to his house, the wind blowing cold in their faces, his placid smile frozen in space and time.

Those same smiling lips came close to a grimace now as she left her Colt and took a few tentative steps towards him, as though her legs were encased in cement.

"What's going on? You look like you've seen a ghost." The concern in his voice made her look up.

"Your ex. She has my number." Emily passed her phone to Ben and waited for his response.

The expression on his face didn't change as he read the message. "It's a lie," he said finally. "I did go to visit my father's grave today, but she wasn't with me. I just got back. Did you pass anyone on the way in?"

"No. No one."

"There, you see. A lie. There's only one way out of here. You would have run into her if she'd been with me." Ben passed the phone back to Emily but he didn't return her gaze. He looked away, then turned and walked into the house leaving the door open behind him.

Emily wanted to drop it, but there were too many questions popping in her head. She followed him inside.

"Then how did she know?"

"I don't know. You'll have to ask her."

"I don't have her number. And come to think of it, how did she get mine?" Emily sat on the rattan chair beside the sideboard but she didn't take off her boots.

"I guess she saw your number on my phone. I have a landline in the office. Caller ID. I allowed her to come and get the rest of her things out when it looked like you and I...," he faltered. "When it looked like you might stay over. It appears she took more than I would have allowed. I wasn't here."

"Why? Were you afraid she wouldn't leave? You never did ask her to go. You said it yourself." Emily stifled a sob. "Are you...are you still in love with her?"

"No, oh no. Emily, please don't cry. We've nothing between us. Not for a long, long time. She's playing games, that's all. I can put a stop to it, but I will have to meet with her, face to face. I guess I've been avoiding the inevitable. I'll take care of it this coming week, okay?"

Emily wanted to believe him. Above everything else, as he undid her laces and put her boots away. With every core of her being, as he eased the cleansed moccasins over her slender feet.

She wanted to believe that Doris was ancient history. But was she? Woman's intuition. Hillary swore by it. Caitlyn wore it like a permanent tattoo. She didn't know why, but somehow things didn't come easily to her. No amount of intuition had guided her in making a decision. When she determined to do something, she simply went ahead and did it. Feelings came after the fact, smug satisfaction or heated self-abasement depending on the outcome.

Right now, the only thing she felt was numb. But Ben was comforting her, attending to her immediate needs and she didn't want him to stop. Suddenly, he grabbed her by the arms and pulled her to her feet, forcing her to look at him.

"I want you." He was emphatic when he bent and breathed into her ear.

"I want you too," she whispered back. Then she threw her arms around him and held on, as if afraid to let him go.

Chapter Twenty-five

The next week dragged on like the horrid weather. By Friday evening, incessant cold rain and high winds kept most of Bangor's fold inside. She supposed its sensible residents would be hunkering on sofas beside snack bowls in front of their televisions and game systems, praying for the power to stay on.

Emily prayed she wouldn't go off the road, or be struck by a flying cow. Storms had been a lifelong fear. Still, she ignored the patrol warnings to stay inside and kept on course all the way to Ben's.

She had promised him a copy of the hunting story, hot off the press. While the magazine issue was still in production, her article was written, the page layouts complete, photos in place. Emily knew it was her best work to date. Especially since Tyrone had been impressed enough to give it a literary nod.

"So, you don't wish one of the boys had done this story? You liked it that much!" Emily had eyed him suspiciously.

"Good God no, girl." He'd given her a most paternal pat on the back. "You were starting to look a little run down and pallid. I was hoping you'd get out to enjoy some fresh country air. I wasn't worried about your writing. I'm sure you could write a story about snowstorms and sell it to the Eskimos. Shall we have a drink to celebrate your nomination for the Ellie award?"

Emily thanked her chief of command, but declined. "I have to get an early start tomorrow. Deadlines!"

She was dancing with joy and couldn't wait to tell Ben. Spirits still running high, Emily wasn't about to let the bad weather dampen her mood, or keep her from her destination. She would just take her time. Her good, sweet nerve-wracking time. And be cautious. Two hours later, her throat desert-dry from babbling to keep her nerves in check, she reached the Blackheart domain.

Ben stood like a monolith on the veranda letting the harsh wind and sleet slash over him. When Emily's lights cut the inky blackness, his pulse quickened. A deep breath seared his throat. *Emily, thank God.*

She ran to him and he whisked her inside.

"The warnings were televised, on radio, social media for Christ's sake! What are you doing out driving in this? We could have waited. *You* should have waited for a break in the weather." His words came out harsh, surprising them both.

He looked away. If she hadn't scared him witless. The past hour...he'd been in pain, physical pain, not knowing what had happened.

"I didn't think the full brunt of the storm had come. Not that I've driven in much worse, but it really wasn't that bad. I just took my time and drove extra slow. I missed you."

Ben knew she was trying to downplay her risky behavior. His glare softened when she lowered her eyes. "May I please have a drink of water? My throat is raw?"

"Got it." Ben left and came back with a glass of water before Emily had time to put her boots away.

"Thank-you." She downed the contents. "Much better."

"Emily?" He took the glass and laid it on the sideboard.

"Yes?"

"I'm sorry. I didn't mean to raise my voice. Forgive me, darling." Ben didn't want the weekend ruined. She was safe now. Why waste two perfectly good days when they could be having fun, making wonderful memories? Then he could reminisce over their time together, conjure her image to fill the void that occurred each Sunday evening when she left his home.

A weak smile offered hope. "I was going to forgive you. But first I want to get out of these soaking wet clothes. I'm much better at accepting apologies when I'm not cold and wet." Emily hadn't stopped shivering since she left her car.

"Come on then, follow me."

They penguin-walked to the bedroom, trying their best not to drip on the furniture. Then they shed their clothing and left them on the floor in a heap before plunging inside the warm bedding. As it turned out, Emily did forgive Ben, long before she was dry again.

The following weeks did not drag by. Emily, unleashed from the pressure of not having a deadline with American Outdoorsman, pressed on with her renovation work. Ben joined in and gave several helpful suggestions towards making the home more energy efficient. She'd also been able to meet him for lunches at The Hungry Owl when he came to town for household supplies and Ava's medications.

Taking a rare evening off from Ben and her renovation work, she was catching up on the local gossip with Caitlyn and the housework in the apartment they shared. Caitlyn was on dish duty again.

"How long has it been now?" she asked, blowing a glob of bubbles off a drinking glass in her hand. The glob landed on the breakfast bar beside Emily's open laptop. "Oops."

Emily smeared the soap bubbles off with the palm of her hand and grabbed a sheet of paper towel from the roll beside her. "Almost three months, though it seems like much longer. The time just seems to be flying by. Ava is already talking about spring and going to Presque Isle for a month or two."

"Ben's mother? Must be a pain to have her there all the time."

"You would think, but no. Ava is still quite active for an old gal. Friday morning bingo, bridge Wednesday evenings and frequent visits to friends and to her church. She does come to have supper with us, and we sometimes join her for a cocktail in the evening, but it's never a bother. Actually, she's rather sweet, if you can get past her bluntness. I guess at her age though, she's entitled to speak her mind. I know she means well."

"Well, I'm happy for you. What have you planned for this weekend? I want to do some last minute Christmas shopping and I need your help." Caitlyn unplugged the sink and carefully sprayed the last of the bubbles down the drain angling the nozzle away from her friend's computer.

"Wood," the single word dropped out of her mouth, no doubt leaving Caitlyn to wonder why on earth she found the country life so appealing.

Not that it was doing her any harm. Trudging through snow swept woodlots, dragging logs out of the forest with Ben, added muscle and tone to Emily's physique that no amount of running had accomplished. It also explained her weight gain, relieving that bit of anxiety.

She was radiant, happy and for the first time, in love. She hadn't been bothered by any unwanted phone messages either. Doris seemed to disappear as suddenly as she had arrived. Ancient history – finally.

Ben wasn't pleased with Emily's decision to forgo their Friday night, but he had to give her some leeway. Caitlyn needed her after all. Friends helping friends. He got that.

Besides, they still had Saturday night, and though there was snow in the forecast, he'd made sure Emily's all-season tires were switched over to snows and she did have a winter tune-up done on her car. He'd insisted on those precautions and taken care of them himself.

Ben also wanted to broach the subject of her moving in with him again, or at least spending more time there than just weekends. Hadn't she swooned over the peace and tranquility?

"Ben, are you still there?"

"Sorry darling, I was wondering what to do with myself. Well, you two have fun. And if you see anything you like, make a note of it. I'm clueless as to what you want for Christmas. You could help me out a little. I'd hate to disappoint you," he spoke in earnest into his phone.

"I have all I want, Ben. And I'm not really much of a shopper. I'd live in Hillary's hand-me-downs if it meant never having to buy new clothes and accessories. I would like to pick up something nice for your mother though. Is there anything particular you know of that she would like?"

A grandchild, thought Ben, but he didn't think it the appropriate time to bring that up. "She likes scarves," Ben answered. He was touched by her thoughtfulness.

"I'm hesitant about that. All old ladies get scarves for Christmas. Mostly because the givers of such presents lack imagination. I'll find something. Look, I have to go. I'll see you tomorrow evening. I shouldn't be too late."

"You're already late. But, I guess I can let your friend have you to herself for one day. See you tomorrow. Kisses."

Chapter Twenty-six

What was he thinking? Emily was Christmas shopping for *his* mother and he hadn't gotten her a single thing. Ben broke the tip of his pencil tapping it on the side of the drafting table, but instead of reaching for the sharpener, he picked up his phone. Just a quick text to let her know he may be a little late getting home. An errand to run. He added a smiley face and pressed send.

Emily shared his displeasure in ogling department store windows and hedging through throngs of harried shoppers. He wondered if part of the reason for that was because she could afford so little herself. She always seemed to struggle with her finances, not knowing whether to pay a bill or spend the money on herself when she needed a manicure or could use a day at the spa.

Ben wanted to take all those worries away from her. But what could he offer that wouldn't encroach on her independence? Something she guarded well by not talking about her circumstances. Any time she hinted at a shortcoming, or something she felt she could put off for another day, he had wanted to come through and make the problem disappear with the stroke of his pen. It would be that easy for him.

Only he didn't believe she would allow it. She fought with him over the expensive tires he insisted on buying for her car, reasoning that if it were not for him, she'd really have no need of them. He left no room for argument there. Other than the rubber,

Emily hadn't let him buy her more than lunches and a few cups of coffee.

Still, she never turned up at his home empty handed. Ben took the extra apple pie that she made out of the freezer and placed it on the counter to thaw. She'd picked the last of the season's crop herself intent on proving that her baking skills were not imaginary. They would enjoy this one later in the evening snuggled beside each other in front of the fireplace.

Ben glanced outside taking in the flakes of snow that had started to fall. Perhaps they'd have a white Christmas that year. Only three days left. He grabbed his coat, an unexpected feeling of peace and reassurance sweeping over him. He knew what he had to do.

Ben could barely contain his joy when he saw the chunky tire tracks in the snow leading into his property. Plumes of smoke chugged out of the chimney when he reached his cosy abode. As he pulled in beside Emily's small blue Colt, he imagined her curled up with Jack by the fire waiting for him to come home.

A small black and gold bag tied with ivory ribbon lay on the seat beside him. He wondered if he would he be able to keep this secret from the woman he loved for three more days. He opened his glove compartment and tucked the bag inside.

The mouthwatering aroma of fresh perked coffee and warm apple pie greeted Ben when he entered through the back porch loaded down with seasoned hardwood. His smile grew when he noticed the near full wood box. He dropped his load and kicked off worn wary leather boots. Hanging his faded denim jacket on one of the wall hooks, he realized Emily must have filled the box herself. Was there anything she wouldn't or couldn't do? Ben wondered.

A picture of her in the Highlands came to mind. Emily wielding a ten pound axe over her head, trying her best to hit the middle of a maple log on the chopping block. Watching her miss and almost strike herself with the blade on several occasions had put knots in his stomach.

But she persisted, listening to his snippets of advice until she was hitting her target with a high measure of accuracy.

She exhibited the same tenacity when learning to drive the Polaris. Wrenching the cumbrous vehicle over boulders and gullies, narrow tree-lined paths rife with thick exposed tree roots, over hill and dale, until the muscles in her two slender arms burned with exertion. She'd been so adaptable, expressing total joy and exhilaration in their many outings.

Her drive reminded him of Ava. Perhaps he should go get her. Other than daily visits from Rosie, Ava had no social agenda for Saturday evenings. Before Emily, he'd spent most of those times with her at the farmhouse, watching documentaries on her favorite television station or the occasional movie that piqued her interest.

They would savor a glass of scotch and before she finished her second she would switch on *The Bachelorette*, giving Ben the excuse to take his leave. Jack would decide then whether to make the effort to follow his master home or stay curled in the comfort of Ava's fire.

Ben swung open the inner door to the kitchen and stepped inside. "Smells good in here. Where are you?" he called out.

Soft light filled the kitchen. An assortment of candles burned on a large pewter plate in the middle of the kitchen table. Sprigs of holly with bright red berries surrounded the plate's rim. Ben hadn't done any decorating for the season. He didn't recognize the centerpiece.

"We're in here," a prompt reply came from the living room.

Next, he heard Jack's tail thumping on the thick Persian rug. His head rest against Emily's silken lap. Candles glowed from the mantel above. Emily lounged in front of a well-tended fire.

"Don't move," he ordered when she began to shift position. He went to his office and returned seconds later with a small digital camera. "I want to take your picture, darling."

She was scantily clad in midnight blue silk, her long auburn hair swept over one shoulder. With firelight dancing in somber brown eyes and bathing her in a soft, warm glow, she had never looked more beautiful. He took several photographs, then laid the camera on top of the mantel.

"Come to me. I can't wait any longer," she purred. Her sultry voice brought him to his knees. She reached for him, allowing Jack to rise and escape the heat of the room.

Ben dropped to his knees and stretched out beside her, taking her in his arms and burying his head in her cleavage, flicking off small beads of perspiration with his tongue. Her moan sent sparks through his veins, igniting his desire with animalistic intensity. She arched her back allowing a thin strap to slip from her shoulder and her breast to escape the deep cut and flimsy fabric of her negligee.

The pie and coffee were tepid at best by the time they finished making love. A gleaming bed of coals lay in the hearth, a sizzling backdrop to the sated and drowsy couple laying naked on the living room rug.

"This feels so good," said Emily. "I could never tire from being here." She felt warm and protected in his arms, his considerable strength perceptible even in this most relaxed state of being.

"I hope so," said Ben. "I'm glad you changed my mind."

Emily propped herself up on an elbow and peered down at his quirky grin. "How so?"

"I was going to get mother and bring her back for the evening. But when I saw you were here, I decided mother could wait. I think she'd understand. In fact, she would probably be delighted to know someone has finally captured my heart. She's a soft spot for you already, I can tell."

"Well, I'm glad I caught your attention. It would have been quite the waste of time for you to go to her. She left a note on your door on her way to Francine's. She's gone for the night and not to be expected until tomorrow morning after church."

"Perhaps she thought to get out before the snow hampered her way." Ava's change in routine didn't send up a red flag, but he worried about her comings and goings. Especially in the winter months. "Or I guess she could have gone to Francine's to give us some privacy."

"I told you, she's a darling, darling." Emily rose and feeling the cooler air give gooseflesh to her bare arms, ran to the bedroom. Ben stretched lethargically, not ready to relinquish the feelings of warmth and contentment that lingered.

Emily flicked on the bedroom light and closed the door to retrieve their bathrobes from a two-pronged hook – a recent installment. She slipped into her own and ran back to find Ben sprawled on his side on the sumptuous rug.

"I guess I can't call this virgin wool anymore," he sighed, smoothing his hand through the creamy undyed fibers, where Emily lay just moments ago.

She tossed the black robe over his head and laughed heartily. "No doubt there are other innocent pieces of décor you'd like to defile, or have you had your fill for the night?" she teased. "I must tell you though, I'm running low on energy. And if you don't get up, I'm going to eat this whole pie by myself."

Regarding the neglected tin plate on the coffee table she picked up the pie and spun towards the kitchen flashing bare legs and buttocks behind her.

"Very cute," murmured Ben with an appreciative smile.

But the flashing came from the middle of her floor-length robe, and as she grappled for the tie that hung from its loops, her fingers caught in the slit that she hadn't noticed.

"Hey, what's this?" The puzzled expression on her face mirrored Ben's as he stood and went to her shrugging his own robe over his shoulders.

Emily lit the kitchen and shoved the pie on the table. She took off her robe and spread it open revealing a slice in the terrycloth fabric that ran from the waist to the top of the hem. Her gasp startled Ben as he entered. Then he stiffened, seeing the full extent of the damage.

"How could this happen?" Her voice trailed off with anguish.

"Perhaps it's worn out. It may have come apart in the wash last time you laundered it." Ben took the robe and laid it on the counter. He wrapped his own around Emily, a shivering waif, the back of her head a damp, tangled mass.

"I would know. I wear it all the time when I'm here. And I haven't washed it lately."

Ben had come to the stark conclusion that someone, for some reason, had symbolically stabbed her in the back. He knew the one person who would do such a thing. But that meant Doris had been in his home. From the look on Emily's face, she had figured that much out herself.

Feeling vulnerable he went to the bedroom for a pair of pajama bottoms. Ben didn't know how to answer her interrogative stare. He came back to the kitchen, went to the porch for an armload of wood and breezed past her on his way back to stoke the fire. It promised to be a chilly night. He could sense frost already forming in the corners of Emily's mind.

"Why aren't you saying anything?" She stormed after him.

"What could I say? You already look like you've made up your mind that I'd done something wrong."

The truth in his words stymied her anger. Emily's expression softened. She'd never been one to exercise emotion by jumping to conclusions and hurling accusations. Only no similar experience had prepared her for this.

Maybe she didn't know how to react, but she knew she didn't want to fight with the man she loved three days before Christmas. She followed him into the living room.

"You're right. I'm sorry."

Ben dropped his armload of wood on the hearth by the fire. "You have nothing to feel sorry for. You did nothing wrong. And neither did I, although I think now that I did a rather poor job of letting Doris know that my home was off limits. Are you sure you're okay?"

"Yeah, I think so. Could we just go to bed? I need you to just hold me tonight."

"Good idea. We can talk."

Ben had been up at dawn to replenish the fire and plowed the full length of their private lane before Emily's cold toes hit the bedroom floor. When he came inside to let her know that he still had to clear Ava's driveway and shovel off the front steps, Emily was dressed, in the kitchen and pounding on a bag of frozen blueberries with her fist.

"Need a hand?" He knew a solid mass of berries didn't stand a chance of nixing her plans to use them if that was her intention.

"I can manage." She flashed him an appreciative smile, dropped the bag in the sink and came to give him a good morning kiss. "I'm going to make pancakes for breakfast. We have everything here I need. It would have been nice to have maple syrup, but the blueberries will make them tasty enough."

"I don't doubt you. I'll grab some from mother's pantry just the same, after I get her cleared out. Can you put everything on hold for just another half hour?"

Emily glanced at the frozen bag and scowled. "I'm sure I can."

He kissed her before setting out again.

"Great! See you soon."

As Ben shoveled the last remnants of snow off the deck in front of her door, Ava's car pulled into her yard. "Good timing, mother!" He took her cane and helped her out of the car, up the stairs, into her home.

"Brrrrr, it's cold," she lamented. "Be a dear, Benny and bring in my parcels for me. They're in the trunk. No peeking."

He left to do her bidding, returning a minute later laden with shopping bags. "I hoped you wouldn't bother with Christmas shopping this year. There really isn't any need for it."

"There's no reason for me to shave my legs anymore either, but I still do it religiously," she said with a chuckle.

"Always a lady. I have to admire you, mother."

"Speaking of ladies, how are you and Emily doing?"

Ben was happy for the change in conversation. He'd no interest in discussing his mother's personal hygiene and he could tell she wished to distract him from the parcels he'd set down on the kitchen table.

"We're doing fine. Are you sure you want to stay home during the holiday? The Grafton's are really nice people."

"I'm sure her family would understand my wishes."

The plan was for Emily to spend Christmas Eve with Hillary, Joe and Finnegan. From Christmas evening until the first week of January, her holiday would be spent with Ben. The Graftons had wanted Ben to come as well, but he wouldn't leave his mother alone. She refused to consider coming along when an invitation was extended to her.

Ava explained that her first Christmas without Donald, she needed to be in their home. His spirit would want her there. She'd already planned to visit the gravesite Christmas morning. Ben knew she had no qualms about lacing on snowshoes to achieve the task if that's what it would take.

Sitting at her kitchen table on Sunday morning, she portrayed equal assertion when he quizzed her about Doris. "I have no idea what you're talking about, Benny. I haven't seen a shadow of her since I hurt my ankle."

"I know she's been in my house. I just want to make sure you didn't have anything to do with it." Besides Emily, she was the only person who had a set of keys to the new locks he'd installed in the entry doors, more for Emily's peace of mind than his own. "If you're in cahoots with her, I want to know now, mother. If this doesn't stop I'm afraid I won't be able to keep Emily coming back. She's scared stiff. And who wouldn't be?" he added with heated breath.

"I have no idea how she got in your house, Benny. But, really now. I'm sure there's nothing to be frightened about. I wouldn't give such childish antics any credence. When, do you suppose, did Doris do this outlandish deed?" She seemed to accept without question that only one person could be responsible.

As much as he hated to admit it, Ben had no idea when his former girlfriend had last been in his house. It could have been after he left on Saturday. The snow would have covered her tracks. They'd had little but rain and flurries before then and Ben's trained eye would have picked up on her low profile tire treads. Unless he'd been distracted and missed them.

Right now Emily was in his kitchen making blueberry pancakes for them and he was missing her already. "Are you sure you won't come for brunch? Blueberry pancakes hot off the griddle! I'm completely out of maple syrup though."

"I had breakfast with Francine before church, thank-you. We were up late talking and watching a movie. I'd rather take a nap right now. Perhaps I'll join you later for supper." Ava went to a cupboard and took out a pint sized jar half filled with golden liquid. "Here, will this be enough?"

"Plenty, thank you." Ben leaned over and kissed her thinly lined cheek. "I'll check in on you later."

Ben tucked the slim amber bottle inside his jacket pocket and left, conscious of a dull aching throb in his temples. He laid blame on the bright, post-storm sun reflecting off a blanket of snow that cloaked their adjoining properties. Squinting, he jumped on the ATV, now equipped with a snow blade, and backed down the lane.

The throbbing intensified when he strode in through the back door and stripped off his cold, wet clothes. A bag of flour, some bowls, milk and eggs, sat seemingly abandoned on the kitchen counter. He found Emily in the front foyer, struggling into her boots.

There were daggers in her eyes when she looked up at him. "Doris sent me a text. Only it's not a message for me."

Ben dropped the bundle of wet clothes in his hands and took the phone from her trembling outstretched hand.

"It's a text conversation you had with her that she cut and paste, then sent to me." Her voice was dead cold.

He read the words on the screen twice to make sure he could believe what he was seeing.

Doris, please talk to me.

What is there to talk about? Leave me alone.

Please. You know I love you and I'd never do anything to hurt you.

Perhaps we should meet.

I'll leave now.

Ben was ashen. "I can explain."

"You don't have to explain anything. This says it all, doesn't it?" Emily snatched her phone out of his hand and whirled around. She was frantic, blind with rage as she grasped her purse and yanked her coat off a hanger, sending it flying across the parquet floor. She left without doing up her boots, slugging through the snow, tears streaming down her face.

Ben was in shock. He stood there, riveted to the floor, holding his breath. Emily was swishing the thick layer of snow from her windshield with the arm of her coat. Then he watched her sharp retreat, the zigzag of her tires spinning in the snow, leaving a thick spray of slush in her wake.

Breathe, damn it...move! Go after her! His thoughts screamed.

Keys, where are my keys? Silly how the brain shuts down at the most dire of times. If Ben had stopped for a second to think while he grabbed clothing – briefs, socks, shirt and pants, a pair of dry boots – he would have realized that his keys were hung on a small brass hook on the wall in the back porch where he'd been hanging them with rigid regularity. But he forgot.

Ben hadn't cleared off his Jeep either and to his chagrin, had parked the ATV behind it before heading to the back door. They were going to cut a Christmas tree on one of his woodlots after breakfast and use the Polaris to haul it out, so he hadn't bothered to put it away.

By the time he climbed into his Jeep and tore down the lane, Emily was long gone. He'd reached the top of the service road before realizing he had no hopes of catching up to her.

He struck the steering wheel with clenched fists, letting a torrent of curses escape his sun and wind burnt lips. Then, with a sinking heart, he turned around and made his way back home, the beauty of the snow laden countryside imperceptible through a blur of dark thoughts and tears.

Chapter Twenty-seven

Emily lost herself in the sinking sun. Its rays cast coral and cherry pink glances off scattered puffs of white. To her left, under a cerulean sky, a band of dark menacing clouds clutched the horizon. Emily didn't know whether to laugh or cry. A nervous snicker welled up inside her.

I'm going crazy. No!

The strain was getting to her, she reasoned. All the questions. Who did what? When? Why? There were no answers. It didn't matter. It was over. She replayed the events of the past few months over and over in her mind. What choice did she have in leaving?

Doris wanted Ben back and in some way, he had given in to her. Hadn't he defended Doris each time she did something that was meant to hurt her? Things that would have sent any sane woman, anyone with an ounce of self-respect, or intuition, fleeing.

She'd been a fool. A crazy, love-struck fool. A flood of tears streamed down her cheeks. She had no strength to fight them back. No fortitude to fight her rival either. *"You win. YOU WIN, BITCH!"*

Caitlyn arrived home a moment later, missing the near mental breakdown. Emily was grateful, but she still couldn't hold back the tears.

"There, there. Come sit down and tell me what's wrong." Caitlyn slipped out of a bear hug and shrugged off her winter attire. She motioned Emily to the cushy, crimson sofa, which now resembled the swell and color of her eyes, and pat her knee. Emily acknowledged the gesture and stretched out, laying her head in Caitlyn's lap.

Caitlyn smoothed errant wisps of hair away from Emily's tear-stained cheeks as she vented.

"He's a rat," Emily mused. The last of her tears finally in check.

"A scoundrel," Caitlyn retorted. "He doesn't deserve you."

"He's a lying, cheating jackass."

"The worst kind."

"A bully too. Always having to have things *his* way."

"Absolutely. No less than a tyrant. I could tell the way he looked at you."

"Possessive, too. You should see the way he looks at me sometimes."

"I thought I just…" Caitlyn stopped midsentence. "Isn't that your phone ringing?"

Emily rolled off the lap of her confidant and sat up. "You can check to see if it's Hillary if you want. I'm not accepting any calls from him."

"How many times has he called?"

"Only twenty. If that's him again it will make twenty-one."

"Well, you must have something to say to him. It's almost Christmas after all."

Emily shot a glance at Caitlyn that was as efficient as any bullet. A dead subject, don't bring it up.

"I don't know what else to say. I'm sorry. I was going to ask you for a drive to the airport, but I think I'll just call a cab. You know I'm going to Boston for a week to spend Christmas with my parents. I suggest you spend the time with your family as well. I know they're no substitute for me, but I guess they'll have to do."

Emily knew her friend was trying to cudgel a smile out of her before she had to leave. It broke her heart even more seeing Caitlyn go, but she did manage to offer a weak grin.

"And don't give that horrid man and his squaw a second thought. She deserves to be shot and dragged down the tarmac behind a Boeing 747.You're too good for him. I'm sure you're Prince Charming is just around the corner. You have to kiss a lot of frogs first you know." She finished on a note of authority.

Emily winced. She would never have referred to Ben's ex with such a derogatory term. To her the word 'squaw' held the same stigma as the N-word when referring to Afro-Americans. She did however like the idea of dragging the hateful woman behind the back of an air bus. There, her hurt had turned to anger. In some way that revelation gave her strength.

"Come on, girlfriend. I'll drive you to the airport." She went into her bedroom and brought out a small box wrapped in fuchsia colored paper and topped off with a bright purple bow. "Do you have room for this in your luggage?"

Caitlyn took the box and smiled. "How thoughtful. I can't imagine how many lunch breaks you gave up to find my favorite hues, as untraditional as they are. Thank you."

They hugged a long while, both women savoring the comfort it provided. "I left yours under my bed with the dust bunnies. I was going to call you and tell you where it was before you left for Portland. I hope you like it."

"I'm sure I'll love it, same as always." The tears began to well again, but Caitlyn's smirk paired with a look of sheer glee in her sparkling blue eyes quelled the need to cry. Taking a deep breath she followed her friend into the bedroom to get the two suitcases lying in wait.

Emily knew that one of them would return with a different horde of gifts than those that were presently on their way to Boston. She shut the door behind them, not bothering to turn off the light that Caitlyn flicked on when she came home to get her luggage.

Ben had never looked or felt so haggard. He couldn't sleep and he felt hollow inside. The hollowness may have been due to the fact that he'd lost his appetite – it had been days since he ate a decent meal. It didn't help that neither of the women who hated him would answer or return his calls.

He was furious with Doris. Whatever he had done to hurt her could never be undone. And now he could never forgive her for taking such extreme measures to get rid of Emily. Still, he felt sorry for her since her revelation when she agreed to meet him at Sam's Pub.

"Social anhedonia? Are you sure?" Ben hadn't studied psychology, but he knew from previous behavior that what the doctor told her must be true. He had seen her in states of gloom that no amount of understanding and compassion could break through. There were moments of real joy as well, but those were infrequent and fleeting, never lasting for any appreciable length of time.

Doris nodded her head and passed him a copy of her prescription.

"I'm glad you finally decided to see a doctor who was able to give you a sound diagnosis. With treatment I'm sure you'll be fine. But I can't help you anymore." He passed back the white piece of tablet paper. "Since you left...." He stopped to look her in the eye. He had to make her understand. "Since you left, I met someone who I want to start a new life with. And I want you to do the same. You know I'll always care about you, but I can't go back. And neither can you. It wouldn't be fair to either of us."

"Fair?" Her voice seethed with anger. "What's fair about this? I have ten years invested in *us*, Ben. You expect me to just walk away?"

Ben looked around the pub. Her bitterness caught the attention of patrons enjoying a beer and a mid-afternoon meal. It had been a mistake to meet Doris in a public place. She didn't give a rat's ass if people were staring at them or not.

"Doris, please. Let's go for a walk. We have to talk about this."

"I'm leaving." Her chair wobbled noisily on the hardwood slats in her haste to stand up. She stormed outside without looking back.

Ben steadied the chair, threw some bills from his wallet on the table and strode after her. When he caught up to Doris beside the open door of a black Camaro, he stopped and swore.

"Damn it, woman! You have to listen to me. You can have anything you want – anything but the land and the house. You want money? Name your price. You can have as much as you want." He paused to catch a breath, his heart pounding in his chest.

"I don't want your money. I want what's mine. And I won't settle for anything less...*sweetheart*." Her words dripped with scorn.

She slammed her door shut, forcing Ben to jump out of the way to avoid being hit with the heavy slab of metal. Then she tore out of the parking lot and disappeared. Could he even hope it would be for good?

We're sorry, but the mailbox for Miss Paige is now full, please try again later.

Ben growled and punched the 'end' button on his phone. He refused to text her. She couldn't trust where it would be coming from. She probably thinks Doris is right here with me flipping pancakes, or worse, thought Ben. He couldn't imagine the horrors that Emily was conjuring up about the two of them. But he knew they were lies, containing no more substance than a breath of stale air. Somehow he had to convince her.

Chapter Twenty-eight

A white Christmas passed. It could have been black for all Ben cared. Most people he knew were overjoyed to see the snow come down. No doubt the white backdrop enhanced all those energy-sucking light bulbs people hung all over the place. He felt like the life had been sucked out of him as well. Nearing the end of the January, not a great deal had changed.

Wearing a thermal shirt and warm sweater under a long oilskin coat, Ben trudged in snowshoes across the frozen landscape. Jack harbored an aversion to deep snow. He had been content to lie in wait in a patch of sunlight on Ava's front porch. Weeks had passed without a hint of sun to penetrate the oppressive winter sky.

Ben didn't need to check on his stand of maple trees. However, he found it impossible to concentrate on the renovation plans he'd been working on, and he'd already split every stick of seasoned wood that needed to be split to heat his home. If it had been closer to spring, he could start to tap the trees and hang small tin pails in preparation of the sweet flowing sap. Still in the rigid grip of winter, he would have to wait.

With nothing much to do besides lament the loss of his Emily, Ben wandered aimlessly through the woods until he found himself at the hunting lodge. He wondered if any snow had managed to drift inside through the cracks where mesh and plaster eroded between the sagging logs. He'd had no desire to go there since Emily left.

Staring now at the derelict building, he was struck by how cold and downtrodden it appeared, somehow reflecting how he felt.

He unstrapped his snowshoes and stepped inside. He expected the cabin to feel like an icebox. It didn't. It took several minutes for his downcast eyes to adjust to the dim light. At first glance, everything appeared to be normal.

Ben was drawn to the gallery wall that he'd hung their picture on – a photograph of them together after she'd finished working on her hunting story, *Meat Lucy*. She had positioned her camera on the table and set the timer so she could settle in beside him on one of the sofas. Ben was beaming, a megawatt smile facing towards the camera lens while she, in profile, looked up at him with adoring eyes. A photo just for him, she'd said.

Only right now, the space that held the picture was blank.

No! His mind reeled. *It was mine. Emily was mine. And I let her slip away.*

When he staggered back from the wall, he nearly tripped over the box of splints and old newspapers next to the woodstove. Newspapers that weren't there, he was sure, the last time he'd been there.

Ben picked up one of the papers, dated two days prior. Had some lost hikers or hunters come across the cabin and taken refuge inside waiting for a break in the weather?

He wrenched open the cast iron door and looked inside. A piece of twisted and melted plastic was all that remained of the frame that he knew held the treasured photo. A single unburned cigarette filter lay beside it. Ben could just pick out the yellow tinged writing that proclaimed its brand. Now he was sure.

Doris!

She was like a ghost haunting him in a dream. But this wasn't a dream, it was real. A real nightmare. Doris hadn't gone anywhere. She'd been right under their noses the whole time. He whipped around and ran to the cupboards, yanking the doors almost off their weary hinges. Nothing there.

He went to the bedroom. An artic sleeping bag lay on one of the bunks. A long smooth bump in the fabric told him something, or somebody, was inside. The steady drip of melting snow pinging off the stovepipe amplified the otherwise eerie silence.

Ben took a tentative step towards it, half expecting the flap to whip open and Doris to fly out of the bag – some ethereal figure, black as night with blistering lumps of coal for eyes – but there was no movement beneath the nylon covered shell.

For a fleeting moment Ben wished he'd brought one of his guns. Then he realized that whatever lay inside the sleeping bag, it was no threat to him. There wasn't a breath of life in whatever it was that lay there. Ben peeled back the top of the bag.

The jackrabbit, he noted, had been dead and frozen for some time. It was one of the largest he'd ever seen. Around its neck a thin wire noose revealed how it met its end. Ben didn't use snares. He thought them inhumane. He didn't hunt for fur. And he shared Emily's dislike of the strong taste so had never hunted them with a rifle either.

He reached down and ran his fingers through the soft fur, came to the noose and felt a scrap of paper under its lifeless head. Ben tore it from the twisted wire and gawked at the familiar scrawl.

Emily – you poor thing.

Panic rose with the bile in his throat. Had Doris gone completely mad? This was no time to wait and see. Ben tore through the door and charged into the woods.

When he reached his Jeep he had stripped to a long sleeved shirt, jeans and boots. His sleeves hung ragtag from crashing through dense, brittle branches. Deep scratches bled in the flesh of his arms and a few, more superficial, across the upper left-hand side of his face. He was drenched in sweat.

Ben didn't know Emily's whereabouts. She could be safe at home, or at her office or in Portland visiting family. She could be on Oak Boulevard. He thought to call, but was afraid whoever he talked to would lie and say she wasn't there. To protect her – from him!

Just five minutes, Emily! Give me five minutes! This time, she had to listen. He'd make sure she knew just how much he loved her.

Unless it was already too late.

Ben swallowed the lump in his throat and pressed on, deciding to check the closest option first – her office building. Being close to four o'clock, he may catch her heading out to beat rush hour traffic, as was her habit. The Hungry Owl would be next. It was just around the corner. He was prepared to drive to Portland if that's what it took. He couldn't take the chance of Doris finding her first.

Emily stared at the little pink line in unabashed bewilderment.

"I'm pregnant?"

"So it appears," deadpanned Dr. Cleaver, taking the small wand and checking it again herself.

Dr. Georgina Cleaver studied the expression on her thirty-two year old patient and sighed. "I suppose your biological clock has been ticking off the wall, but in my practice I find that a lot of women are delaying having babies until their thirties. That was almost unheard of when I interned. Today it's quite common, I assure you. So there's no reason to be alarmed. We'll do an ultrasound of course. Just to make sure everything is okay. Have you started having morning sickness yet?"

"Sickness? I'm sorry. I never expected this. We did take precautions." Emily thought about her trip to the Highlands with Ben and the condoms Caitlyn had slipped into her suitcase. At the time, she'd appreciated the gesture, but didn't intend to use them. But they did end up using them. Had always used them – except for the time, when they'd been too crazed with desire for each other to think sensibly. That gorgeous day outside in the woods. She blushed, the doctor's voice cutting through the memory.

"If you take this requisition form to radiology, they'll make the appointment for you. In the meanwhile make sure you get some prenatal vitamins and start taking them right away. I suspect that you're only about five or six weeks in, but the ultrasound will give us a better idea. With your history of irregular periods, it's hard to tell right now. Any questions?" Dr. Cleaver, put down her pen and clipboard and looked expectantly at the mystified woman sitting in her chair.

Noting the lack of a wedding ring on Emily's left ring finger she added, "If this isn't a wanted pregnancy it may not be too late to abort it."

Emily's hand flew over her pelvic region, a protective reflex. "I want it," she gulped. Feeling a well of tears rising to the brink, she stood to retrieve her coat and purse hanging on the back of her seat. She vowed to restrain them, at least until she was in the privacy of her car. "There's no question. It's my baby. I'm going to have a baby."

The doctor gave Emily a maternal smile. "Well, then, congratulations. You can go home now. And ease up on the running. I know some physicians will condone exercise in any form, but I'm not one of them. Brisk walks will do you fine and you can keep up with the yoga as well. Okay, run along, before you turn into a sprinkler."

A gentle hug, a hand stuffed full of Kleenex, and she was out the door. Dabbing her eyes, still trying to keep her composure, Emily scurried down the corridor, eager to drop off her ultrasound requisition and go home.

Going by the psychiatric department on her way to radiology, she passed a tall native woman with piercing black eyes and short, jet-black hair. Even though her glance was peripheral, she could tell the woman was native. What were the chances? Well, she wouldn't know Doris King if she tripped over her in the hallway and fell into her lap, so she dismissed the notion that it was Ben's ex-girlfriend that she passed. They had never met. Emily returned to scanning the yellow piece of paper she held, still trying her best to process the information overload she had just been trounced with.

Doris recognized Emily from the magazine and the photograph in Ben's hunting lodge. She hadn't expected to see her rival walking the corridor, engrossed in a yellow sheet of paper. What were the chances of meeting her here?

Doris had been trying to tail the woman for weeks, but as Emily didn't seem to have any stringent schedule, hadn't been able to pin her down. Thinking that now, she formed an image of Ben's lover in her mind, tacked to a wall behind glass, like some predatory moth. And that thought made her smile, sinister as it was.

With the stealth of a black widow spider, Doris spun around and followed her prey. Emily wouldn't get away from her this time. No more games of chance.

Chapter Twenty-nine

Ben had not found Emily at the austere office building that housed American Outdoorsman. He had no trouble drawing out a curious throng of her co-workers however, having checked behind every door and cubicle, including the stalls in the ladies' lavatory, before giving up. He supposed it helped, looking like a madman on steroids.

Gloria Steinburg did manage to inform him that Emily had been there, but had taken off earlier in the day for personal reasons. She chased him in flats and a shin-length black and white skirt, which reminded Ben of a penguin, to get the full message across. Ben, grateful that no one had called security, pressed the down button in front of reception.

Just before the elevator door closed behind him, Andy Wong's clipped accent bit the silence and snapped the fixated stares off a dozen faces.

"Should we call someone?"

Ben raked his hands through a mop of sweat soaked hair and punched the lobby button. He should have taken the stairs, but he needed to slow down, to catch his breath, to think. Who would know where Emily was at this moment?

Ben blared his horn – too late. Realizing the car ahead of him wasn't about to cruise through a red light to get out of his way, he took a deep breath. *What am I doing?* It would have been quicker to leave his vehicle at Emily's office building and walk to The Hungry

Owl, but that hadn't occurred to him in time either. He was half tempted to abandon his Jeep then and there when suddenly the light turned green.

Caitlyn stood at the cash register ringing off the day's receipts, preparing to close up. Ben banged three times on the door. He put his ear to the glass.

"If you're going to rob me, you'll have to find your own way in. We're closed for the night. Can't you read?" She pointed to the closed sign in the window. Ben rapped harder on the glass door and Caitlyn finally looked up. "All right, just a minute." Recognition didn't appear in her eyes until she was up to the door.

"Ben!" She slid the deadlock over and let him in. "What's wrong? Is it Emily? You look a fright. Can I get you something? Why are you bleeding?" She would have rambled on had Ben not grabbed her head with both hands and smacked her lips shut so forcefully with his own.

"Thank-you, Cait'...thank-you. I was afraid you wouldn't open the door and I have to find Emily. Please! Do you know where she is?" Ben was sorry to have startled his next-to-new friend, but he considered her co-operation to be a matter of great importance. He didn't have time to answer questions. And he was truly thankful to her for letting him in.

"Well, she did have a late afternoon appointment today. I saw her at lunch."

"Where? Do you think she's still there or would she be home by now?"

Caitlyn looked at him warily. "I don't know if I should tell you. Why do you need to see Emily?"

Ben was desperate. "Caitlyn, I love her. I would never do anything to hurt her. You have to believe me!"

"But you already hurt her, Ben." Caitlyn sounded indignant. "I know it's because of you she's been crying herself to sleep at night."

Her words kicked him in the gut. "I'm really sorry, but it's not what you're thinking. Emily wouldn't let me explain. She wouldn't take my calls or acknowledge my messages. I don't know why I stopped trying. I guess I didn't think she had the same feelings for me. She cut me off. I was lost. Now she may be in danger, and I have to find her. Will you help me?"

Empathy welled. "I guess so. I don't know. She loves you too, Ben. And I can tell you're still in love with her." Caitlyn glanced at her watch. "If you leave now, you might find her at the Victoria Health Institute. She went to see her doctor for a checkup."

"Caitlyn…"

The clap of her hand across his lips stopped him short. "I know, I know…I'm the best!"

"You absolutely are, Cait!" Ben flew out the door feeling a slight measure of relief.

Emily eased into rush-hour traffic intent on getting home in one piece. Make that two pieces, she thought wryly, now that she carried Ben's child in her womb. Caitlyn would be on her way home from work soon. What would she say?

There would probably be enough time to call Hillary with the news. That thought brought a new round of tears to the brink. Hillary would be happy about the baby. But she knew Ben had let her down and that they were no longer a couple.

A couple. That's what they had been. Right now Emily had never felt more alone. She missed Ben so much. Should she call him too? He did have some responsibility in this. It's not something she could hide from him, that's for sure.

They hadn't talked about having children – only the near future, the making of maple syrup in the spring, a trip to see Tommy and Michelle at a Pow Wow early summer and finishing the renovation on the brownstone – together. How could it have all gone so wrong?

Ching-ching! Emily jumped at the sudden interruption to her thoughts. She ignored her phone, intent on hitting the open road before risking an accident by any further distraction. It was bad enough that the roads still had slippery patches, though snowplows had been out before dawn taking care of the most recent blizzard.

She didn't notice the monstrous black car creeping up behind her.

Ben's chest tightened when he saw her. She must be okay. Emily's blue Colt drove out of the medical building's parking lot with no more than ten cars between them. With traffic going the pace of a drunken snail, he had no doubts about catching up to her. He'd just let out a sigh of relief when a driver in one of the cars ahead decided to play good Samaritan, pausing to allow a black sports car into the lane.

Doris...It can't be! But as he gained position in the lane she occupied he saw the plate number and he knew. Doris was following Emily. Ben was quite sure as well that her intentions were less than friendly. Murderously so.

In any event, *he* wasn't going to take any chances. He kept both cars in view as he darted in and out of lanes, shortening the space between them in the web of traffic. He had almost reached them when Emily swerved into the right-hand lane and took the on ramp towards Fenwick Heights. Doris cut off the driver beside her and darted ahead shortening Emily's lead. She made it to the ramp just as Emily rounded the long, wide turn leading onto the highway.

Ben blared his horn to alert the drivers around him. He accelerated and switched lanes as fast as possible without toppling over. His Jeep was no match for Doris's Camaro, but it was just keeping up with Emily, and the love of his life was conscientiously driving the speed limit. Doris would be on her in seconds. Ben leaned on his horn. If only he could get their attention, he may be able to stop them.

Some maniac was blaring his horn on the ramp coming onto the highway. Emily had a twinge of misgiving about the black car speeding up behind her. What the hell was going on? She glanced behind to see if she could tell where the ruckus was coming from. Her jaw dropped when the sleek sports car sped up and hit her rear bumper.

What's happening?

Emily stomped on her accelerator, bringing her speed up to ninety miles per hour. Gaining some distance, she glanced into her rearview mirror. It couldn't be! Ben's red Jeep cruised up behind the black car. His horn blared again.

The muscle car sped up. Another jolt. Emily's stomach roiled. Now she was feeling sick. She gunned her engine. One hundred miles an hour and the car behind clung to her like a shadow. She knew it could outrun her gutless little Colt with ease. Why didn't it just pass her? And what was Ben doing? Following her? Had he somehow found out she was pregnant? Impossible. She only now found out herself.

Emily scanned the road ahead for the closest off-ramp. At this speed, she might not survive – her baby might not survive – an accident. Incensed, she swerved to the right. Tucking in with the slower traffic, the stalker would have to shoot past her in the fast lane.

She glanced to her left expecting to see the monster speed ahead, but the black car was still on her tail. Cutting in, it nearly clipped the maroon colored truck that Emily slipped in front of.

Horns blared from all directions.

WHAM!

The force of contact bashed her into the steering wheel.

"Ben! Help me!"

Emily trembled like a leaf in a windstorm. When she dared to take her eyes off the pavement and glance in the rearview mirror, Ben's Jeep came into view. The black car had swerved up beside her. She dared a glance at the driver.

Bold black spheres glared back at Emily accompanied by a triumphant leer. What was she doing? Emily's mind raced.

Doris! It had to be.

Fear surged like a steamroller, grinding over her with inexorable force. The next off-ramp was still out of sight. Emily's breathing resembled a woman in labor. Short quick breaths escaped her swollen lips.

Dear God, don't let me pass out!

Ben wracked his brain. He had to stop Doris! But how? They approached a wide turn, wrapped in a corrugated metal guardrail. A ravine led down to snow-covered fields. The nearest off-ramp was still several miles away. He shot ahead of the maroon truck and kept his pace. Motorists honked at him to pass.

Doris whipped her head backwards and glared at Ben. Her Ben! And, now he was going to stay that way. She would slam that little blue car through the guardrail, into the ravine and Emily would smash, roll and crumble away like a thin-shelled bug.

Gone!

She gunned her engine swerving madly ahead of Ben. In seconds she drew alongside of the little blue car again. One good ram and she would send Emily flying...for good!

Ben felt the Jeep wobble as he cut sharply into the left lane. He reached the bumper of Doris's car as it pulled up alongside Emily. A stream of traffic pulled up behind them, horns blaring wildly from harried drivers making their way home. Terror gripped him when he saw Doris swing her steering wheel hard to the right.

The woman in that car must be bat-shit crazy. Emily saw it coming. She hit the brakes. Braced for impact.

The Camaro, still picking up speed, managed to clip her front fender, knocking the Colt sideways. Rubber screeched on pavement as she fought with the steering wheel to gain control and keep from smashing into the guardrail.

Seeing Ben's Jeep steer into the path of Doris's car as they rounded the turn, she screamed. The force of both vehicles, locked in a deadly embrace, sent them crashing through the metal guardrail. In the rearview mirror she watched in horror as the red Jeep flipped over the bank and disappeared.

"Ben!"

Her car finally spun to a stop, facing a barrage of traffic, but braced against the guard rail, safe from the rush of oncoming vehicles. It was a wonder no one else hit her. Sirens filled the air when Emily, still trembling, opened her car door.

"Are you alright, dear?" An elderly man asked, fraught with concern. Several motorists had stopped to offer assistance.

Emily bobbed her head. "I think so, but my...my...his Jeep went over...Ben!" The words ripped from her throat. Tears sprung to her eyes.

Emergency vehicles began to arrive. Three police cars and an ambulance pulled up ahead of her. A fourth police cruiser came to a halt in front of Emily's banged up Colt.

She stepped out of the car. Ignoring the pleas of several voices, she broke into a run. After scrambling over the twisted shards of metal, Emily skid down the bank towards the Jeep leaving a deep furrow of powdered snow in her wake.

By some miracle Ben's vehicle had flipped a full three hundred and sixty degrees, landing back on its wheels, then rolled to a stop. The black Camaro rolled several times until it came to rest rubber side up. It lay on its back, a pale red stain spreading over its chassis.

Doris lay crumpled inside her car, broken and shaky, but alive.

"Help is on its way, Doris. I can't get you out by myself. Don't try to move. Here they come. Hold on now. You're going to be fine. Just fine."

Ben stood and waved at the police and paramedics staring down at the grim scene. A GBN News helicopter swooped overhead. Other media crews were setting up cameras on the highway. Seeing

Emily scampering down the bank, seemingly uninjured, he ran to her.

Several feet stretched between them when she stopped. Ben, still wearing his torn and bloody shirt, soaked in sweat, scratched and chapped, had a bump forming on his forehead. He held her cool gaze as she bent, rolled a ball of snow in her hands and stepped forward. Ben braced himself. She pressed the cold cluster of snow to his forehead.

"Does it hurt?" She was breathless.

"Only the thought of losing you," he gasped. "I was so scared. I couldn't bear to lose you again." He brushed the snow aside and pulled her into his arms. The taste of salty tears ran across their tongues as they locked in a feverish kiss.

Ben carried Emily from the deep snow to the Jeep.

She clung to him like a frightened child. "When I saw you flip out of sight I thought I'd lost you. You could have been killed too. I'm sure my heart skipped a beat when I saw you stand up beside that horrible car."

"That's why I drive a vehicle with a roll cage. In case I ever have to chase after my wife again." Ben opened the passenger side door and gently lowered her into the seat. The glove compartment had come open in the tumble. He picked up the black and gold bag tied with the ivory ribbon that lay at her feet.

He grinned when the meaning of his words registered on her face. "Your wife?"

He pressed the bag into her hand. "That is, if you agree to marry me. I love you, Emily. I want to spend the rest of my life making you happy. And I promise I'll never hurt you again. Say yes...for me, for us."

Emily smiled through her tears. A deep feeling was sweeping over her. It may be a first, but it was one she knew she could trust with all her heart.

"Yes," she murmured. Then her voice rose. "Yes, I'll marry you. Oh, Ben, I love you so much."

Ben opened the bag for her and took out a velvet covered box. The ring inside was magnificent – a white gold band with a large turquoise stone amid a cluster of small diamonds. "It's beautiful," she gushed. "Oh Ben. I'm so happy."

"I'm happy too now, for both of us."

The baby!

"Ben, I have something to tell you. I hope it's something you want as much as I do."

"Now that I have you back, I'll never want for anything again. You're everything to me, Emily. What more could I want?" His brow furrowed.

Then her words sank in. "You have something to tell me?" With his clenched jaw and stern look, he may as well have said "out with it."

"It think you should save that face for your child when he or she grows into a mischievous brat," chirped Emily with as much petulance as she could muster. "I'm due this summer. I don't think it a proper expression to be using on your wife, or future wife as it stands right now."

"Oh! You're pregnant? – we're pregnant!" His eyes became misty again.

"It looks like your mother is going to get her grandchild a little earlier than I planned, but I know I'm ready for a family of my own. The question is, are you? I guess you never considered having children before, but for me, I always wanted a bundle, maybe triplets. Then I'd work from home and look after them all."

She tore her eyes away from him, suddenly afraid of what she was asking. How well did she know him after all? He may have sworn never to have a child. Then what would she do?

Ben turned her face back towards him very gently and kissed her nose. "Put any thoughts aside of having less than four. I always wanted a bundle too. And we'll start with this one right here." He gave her still flat belly a gentle pat.

The whirring blades of the helicopter came menacingly close.

"Let's get out of here. I'll happily concede to you working from home," Ben added thoughtfully. "You'll probably have your hands full with me anyway. By the way, have I ever shown you my writing skills? I wrote a poem for mother once and she loved it."

"Babe?"

"Yes, darling." A new term of endearment. Ben smiled.

"The only thing I want you to show me right now is the way home, before we both freeze to death."

As they trudged up the bank, firemen, equipped with the jaws-of-life, scrambled down towards the squished black car.

"Looks like a lot of blood. Is she dead?" asked Emily through gritted teeth.

"No, it's not blood," said Ben. "Transmission fluid. It appears the pan was almost rusted through. It broke apart when her car rolled over."

The tow trucks arrived next. Ben's vehicle would have to be towed up over the bank. Emily's car was only slightly crumpled and still operable. Ben drove them to the police station to file a report. Home would have to wait. Several eye witnesses had come forward to give statements.

The commanding officer talked about pressing charges of attempted murder against Doris. Ben called the hospital to check on her status and make sure they had her brother's private phone number. He spoke to a doctor, one of his former clients, who provided the information he sought. Ben relayed everything back to Emily.

The deranged woman had been taken to hospital with a concussion, dislocated shoulder, a broken bone in one leg and two broken wrists. She hadn't taken any of her prescribed medications and was experiencing a major psychotic episode at the time of the crash. Her brother, Michael, had been notified and was on his way from Nova Scotia. When Doris was well enough to travel, he could take her home.

Emily was relieved. Ben assured her that with counselling and proper treatment, Doris would not be a problem.

"Can we go home now?" Emily queried, looking into Ben's solemn blue eyes.

An officer overheard her and nodded towards the police entrance door.

"Yes, darling. We can go home now. I'll drive. And you can call mother to give her the good news. She'll be ecstatic."

Epilogue

The Aroostook Pow Wow was in full swing – or full beat, more aptly, Emily thought, listening to the rhythmic pound of drums. In the festive throng everyone on foot appeared to be dancing. There was no shortage of clapping hands and smiling faces either.

They left Uncle John and Ava engrossed in a game of bingo in one of the giant tents set up to facilitate a variety of activities. She and Ben left to look for Tommy and Michelle. It was June and the Blackhearts hadn't seen their friends since Valentine's Day, the day of their wedding. It had been a small private affair with an exorbitant amount of food and good wishes. Ben and Emily couldn't have been happier to exchange vows on the picturesque lake-side estate provided by the Grafton's for their wedding.

Emily didn't need Michelle to tell her fortune anymore. As she patted the swell of her belly, she knew exactly what was in store for her. Still, she was pleased that their friends had decided to come to Maine for this celebration. It wasn't a hard sell. Michelle had relatives on the reservation near Presque Isle and they had been meaning to come for a visit.

Through the swarm, Emily caught the eye of a young native girl in traditional ceremonial dress. A memory from the Cape Breton Highlands washed over her.

"Justine?" The child looked as if she were party to one of the dance troupes. *Would she remember me?*

"Ben," she stopped him and held onto the girl's intense gaze, not wanting to lose her in the crowd. Then the two walked toward each other.

"Justine...is it you?"

"Just Emily! I'm so glad you came to the Pow Wow!" The little girl's smile was infectious. They hugged for several moments.

"Yes, I'm glad too. I was so lucky to find you in the Highlands. And, now, here we are again. You look beautiful!" Emily ran her fingers through the thigh-long fringe that hung from Justine's shoulders. Her white buckskin tunic was heavily beaded and her headdress a crown of eagle feathers. Waves of glossy black hair hung to her waist.

Justine's angelic face had the same almond-shaped eyes, but instead of a timid waif, she appeared every inch a proud lady in the making. "You'll be beating the boys off with sticks in no time!" laughed Emily. "Look at you!"

Ben nodded, then tipped his hat to Emily and signifying that he was heading for refreshments. May as well give them time to get reacquainted. He'd never get a word in edgewise at this point. A smile crossed his face. But tonight. Tonight, he would have Emily to himself. He glanced back. She was following him with her eyes...projecting her love for him through time, space and all that was to come.

The End

Made in the USA
San Bernardino, CA
01 December 2019